ONCE UPON A TIME

SOUTH EAST AUTHORS

Edited by Sarah Washer

First published in Great Britain in 2016 by:

 Young**Writers**

Remus House
Coltsfoot Drive
Peterborough
PE2 9BF
Telephone: 01733 890066
Website: www.youngwriters.co.uk

All Rights Reserved
Book Design by **ASHLEY JANSON**
© Copyright Contributors 2015
SB ISBN 978-1-78443-969-9

Printed and bound in the UK by BookPrintingUK
Website: www.bookprintinguk.com

FOREWORD

Welcome, Reader!

For Young Writers' latest competition, **Once Upon A Time**, we gave school children nationwide the tricky challenge of writing a story with a beginning, middle and an end in just 100 words, and they rose to the challenge magnificently!

We chose stories for publication based on style, expression, imagination and technical skill. The result is this entertaining collection full of diverse and imaginative mini sagas, which is also a delightful keepsake to look back on in years to come.

Here at Young Writers our aim is to encourage creativity in children and to inspire a love of the written word, so it's great to get such an amazing response, with some absolutely fantastic stories. This made it a tough challenge to pick the winners, so well done to Viola Neuls Humphreys who has been chosen as the best author in this anthology. You can see the winning story on the front cover.

I'd like to congratulate all the young authors in Once Upon A Time – South East Authors – I hope this inspires them to continue with their creative writing. And who knows, maybe we'll be seeing their names on the best seller lists in the future...

Jenni Bannister

Editorial Manager

CONTENTS

ST JOSEPH'S CATHOLIC PRIMARY SCHOOL, LONDON

SUNDON PARK JUNIOR SCHOOL, LUTON

WESTFIELDS JUNIOR SCHOOL, YATELEY

THE
MINI SAGAS

Pat 1 To The Rescue

One hot sunny day, Batman, his wife Elsa and six kids all called Pat, went to Mount Everest to cool down. Suddenly, Pat 3 vomited on the magic paper and almost stepped in it. Elsa felt so traumatised because Pat 3 always vomits on air travel. Elsa didn't like the smell of vomit so she just cleaned it up with tissue. All of a sudden, Pats 2, 3, 4, 5 and 6 fell onto the edge of the magic paper. 'Pat 1 to the rescue!' Pat 1 rescued them by using a rope. 'Thank you Pat 1! Thank you!'

Tahmida Ahmed (10)
Bygrove Primary School, London

Snow White And Cinderella's Joyness

Once upon a time in a faraway land, a girl named Snow White saw a magic rainbow. She climbed up the rainbow that had magic. She saw that she was outside the unknown beautiful palace. She went inside and she was trapped! A voice came out from the corner and it was Cinderella. (Oh my God!) 'What are you doing here? You're my childhood friend!'
'I know,' said Cinderella. 'Let's go back to the magic rainbow.'
'Yeah great idea.'
Off they went to have a big feast. After that they played on the swing.

Zahra Rashid (9)
Bygrove Primary School, London

The Hero

One stormy night, the waves swished through! Then the aeroplane crash-landed into the ocean, *poosh*! The passengers couldn't swim so they called for help. Soaring through the sky, out of nowhere Superman appeared! Superman said, 'Superman to the rescue!' The tourists said to Superman, 'Thanks Superman for saving our lives!'
Superman replied, 'No problem!'
The tourists safely made their way back home. When the tourists got home they said, 'There's no place like home, there's no place like home!' Then that very night the tourists had a dream about Superman saving the awe-inspiring world. Superman saved the day today. Wow!

Joseph Kenneth Charles Hutchinson-Pugh (9)
Bygrove Primary School, London

Iceland

One day, in the castle, an invitation came. It said: 'To residents of Wonderland, there'll be a party in Iceland. From the King'.
Elsa shouted, 'Let's go to the party.' Jack Frost got the transformable (you can drive it in the snow). He drove to Iceland.
A fairy said, 'Welcome to Iceland! Don't wake the ice monster!'
Elsa found a hill, she said, 'Let's have a picnic in the hill.'
'Can you feel the movement?' said Jack Frost. With a boom the hill exploded. Elsa screamed. The ice monster chased them all the way to Wonderland inside the crystal ice castle...

Shamema Begum (9)
Bygrove Primary School, London

The Golden Ball

Once there lived a girl, her name was Sally. Sally's sisters never played with her.
One day her dad gave her a golden ball.
The next day when she bounced it, it fell into the fountain. She couldn't reach it until a frog called *Froggy* found it. He said, 'I will give your ball back only if you let me sleep on your bed, eat your lunch and play.'
'Promise,' replied Sally.
Sally's dad opened the door and Froggy said, 'I came to meet Sally.' Froggy slept on the bed, ate her lunch and played. Froggy transformed into a prince.

Alima Begum (9)
Bygrove Primary School, London

The Bushes

One glorious morning Twilight was with her sister Starbright. They played with their brand-new ball. Twilight threw it high, it fell in the bushes. Starbright ran to get the ball in the bushes. A long time passed, Starlight didn't come back... Twilight went to see what happened. She saw blue glows come towards her. She ran to them. She transported into a new world. She felt so panicked. She saw her sister in the middle of the crowd. Then, Starbright ran towards her with the ball. As they touched the ball together, they transported back in front of the bushes.

Ahona Afreen Zaman (9)
Bygrove Primary School, London

Being Kind To Your Friend At Christmas

One snowy morning, it was Christmas and a man called Dantdm and a doctor called Trayaurus were putting up the decorations. Then Doctor Trayaurus gave a present to Dantdm. Dantdm rushed to the lab and opened it. 'Wow you bought me a dog, what shall we name it? Yes, Grim.' So Grim followed everywhere Dantdm went. One day, Doctor Trayaurus made Grim go into the TNT. The TNT exploded and Grim died! A week later, Trayaurus built an invention, put the bones inside and pulled the lever. Grim came back. He wasn't a fur dog, instead a bone dog. Wow!

Shumona Aktar (9)
Bygrove Primary School, London

Michelle, Val And Gosia's Adventure

Michelle, Val and Gosia climbed on their dragon so they could fly to SpongeBob's house. They said, 'Hi,' to SpongeBob.
SpongeBob replied, 'Let's take you on a tour, I'll show you Bikini Bottom.'
Michelle, Val and Gosia were happy to hear this. 'Let's go to Krusty Krabs.' Surprisingly they found Krusty Krabs with broken windows.
Michelle volunteered and said, 'If you feel better we can help clean.'
'I need to find out who did this,' said SpongeBob.
Squidward heard this and said, 'I'll tell you. It's me!' said Squidward.
'Why?' said SpongeBob.
'You're fired!' shouted Mr Krabs.
'Yay.'

Madiha Islam (9)
Bygrove Primary School, London

The Rocket

One dark night, two men named Joseph and John were building a rocket.
The next day the rocket was active. 3, 2, 1, blast-off!
'We are in space!' shouted Joseph. First they saw Pluto (which is not a planet). After that they saw the biggest planet, Jupiter. Suddenly, the rocket broke. But they realised that they were floating. They landed on the cheesy moon, then the moon turned crescent and Joseph and John fell. They shrieked but they landed on Mars. They jumped so high that they landed back on Jupiter. When they accidentally fell they went to Heaven.

Ismail Siddique (9)
Bygrove Primary School, London

Justice League

Long ago there was an evil robot called Darkside.
Batman, Superman, Green Lantern, Flash, Cyborg and Captain Kazzam had to stop him... They were called Justice League.
They circled the town one hundred times until they met Darkside.
Darkside demanded, 'Protect me robot minions!'
'Superheroes attack!' demanded Superman.
Crash! Bang! 'How do we destroy him? We tried using every technology we've got,' moaned Green Lantern and Flash.
'You have to stab the eyes.'
Green Lantern and Flash stabbed the eyes.
'Everyone else distract.'
Kaboom! 'He is down, we are champs! We won, we won,' screamed the team.

Riyad Uddin (9)
Bygrove Primary School, London

Batman To The Rescue

Taryid, Thambir, Tukweed and Tahmid were racing through the clouds, the helicopter chugged away. *Oooo crash!* 'We ran out of petrol!' shouted Taryid. Like a lead balloon the helicopter dropped. They landed on a dormant volcano. Taryid said, 'Let's walk to the top of the volcano.' When they got up to the top of the volcano, the volcano started to rumble. The volcano erupted! Taryid, Thambir, Tukweed and Tahmid ran to their helicopter and drove away. While they were driving the volcano spat on the helicopter and they went flying down, and Batman saved them! They were happily together. Good!

Yusuf Hussain (9)
Bygrove Primary School, London

The Snow Princess

Once there lived a snow princess with a blue dress, she lived in a cottage.
One day an evil witch came when she was asleep and kidnapped her! She put her in a cage! Then she put her in a dungeon and locked it, then her old friend Tweet the bird came. Tweet opened the cage and woke her up. When she found out what had happened Tweet told her if a prince kissed her she would get married. The snow princess said yes. Tweet found a prince, took him to her and he kissed her with magic. They married!

Mishika Khurana (8)
Dunstable Icknield Lower School, Dunstable

A Mad Time In Minecraft

One day in Minecraft in a crazy village there was a boy called Jeffrey. Jeffrey went down in a cave. 'What? A creeper!' said Jeffrey. So Jeffrey went back home.
When Jeffrey got home, 'Jeffrey where have you been?' said Jeffrey's mum.
Suddenly Jeffrey woke up, the paintings were alive! Jeffrey broke the paintings and they were all back to normal. While Jeffrey's mum sat on the settee Jeffrey did the gardening. Soon it was time for dinner. After that it was time for bed. The bed was so comfy. Jeffrey's mum watched the TV so she was really happy.

Summa Molly Topham (8)
Dunstable Icknield Lower School, Dunstable

Dunstable Icknield Lower School Vs Ardley Hill FC

It's the Ardley Hill tournament. DILS FC vs AH FC. They start the match. Harry dribbles the ball quickly and shoots the ball into the goal. DILS FC are winning 1-0. Lewis boots the ball to Caleb and then Caleb dunks the ball into the net. It's 2-0 now and Ethan chops the ball into the air and heads the ball towards the goal. It's 3-0 now. Lewis from AH FC shoots and William does an epic save. Now William boots the ball to Anant and dribbles and passes to Harry. Harry boots and shoots! Now it's 4-0. That's all.

Ethan De-Marro (7)
Dunstable Icknield Lower School, Dunstable

Candy Land

One day in Chile there was a girl called Phoebe who liked to help people. Phoebe was helping a woman cross the road when suddenly she saw a man flying towards her and said, 'You're coming to Candy Land!'
When they got to Candy Land, it was like Phoebe's number one dream, but it was 8.30pm, time for bed. So she went to sleep. When she woke up she had a good look around. Suddenly her foot was stuck. She did not know what to do. She shouted but no one came! What will happen? 'Not this!' shouted Phoebe...

Eloise Bacon (8)
Dunstable Icknield Lower School, Dunstable

The Magic Wardrobe

One scary night, a boy called Danny discovered a magic wardrobe. But let's start from the beginning.
Danny heard a very strange sound coming from the wardrobe. Danny woke up and opened the wardrobe and inside he found a big, fuzzy ball. But it wasn't any ordinary ball it was a fuzzy, big, talking ball! Danny was amazed. He shouted, 'Wow!'
The ball started to talk, 'I'm from space and your wardrobe is magic.'
'How did you get here?'
'My secret.'
Danny took the ball out of the wardrobe. From now on they are best friends for ever.

Anna Karwasz (8)
Dunstable Icknield Lower School, Dunstable

Minecraft

In a forest called Minecraft, there was a man called Steve. When an aeroplane was going past and a storm was heading in the same direction the aeroplane crashed with a *boom!* Only one person survived! He was called Alex. Steve saw Alex. Alex said to him, 'Help me, help me!'
The fire spread like water flowing down a rapid river! Steve looked after Alex, Alex had to live with Steve. November 5th was Alex's birthday. So Steve built Alex a tree house. It was their favourite colours, red and gold. Good times for both of them!

Alex Wallington-Read (9)
Dunstable Icknield Lower School, Dunstable

The Eyes Kept Moving

I'm not sure why the eyes kept on moving. I didn't really know. I was not scared because I'm not scared of anything, and then the elves started to chase me.
After a couple of hours I lost them, then I went home, but they came back to spy on me. I could see them everywhere, they look spooky...

Lewis Hamill (8)
Dunstable Icknield Lower School, Dunstable

The Leprechaun And The Rainbow

Once upon a dream there was a leprechaun called Zac, and his best friend the rainbow, a talking rainbow! Then one terrible day the rainbow faded away and Zac thought he had done something wrong, but it was the evil unicorns who hated rainbows. They were so mean.

Three years later the unicorns took the leprechaun. Everyone cried because the leprechaun was the king, but suddenly a brave tiger came and saved everyone, except the rainbow was trapped. Do you think the rainbow will ever escape?

Savannah Clare (8)
Dunstable Icknield Lower School, Dunstable

The Secret Pony

Long ago, in a cottage near the wild woods, lived a girl called Lily. She always wished to have a pony.

One day, she went into the woods, when suddenly a bush started to glow. Lily ran up to the bush and peered behind it. To her surprise, she found a beautiful unicorn with a silk white coat and a matching mane. Lily slowly stepped close enough to touch it, but the unicorn disappeared. She stared at the spot where the unicorn stood, but nothing happened. She searched everywhere, it just disappeared.

Nicola Barczyk (8)
Dunstable Icknield Lower School, Dunstable

Haunted House

Once, in a small village, a girl called Aimee really didn't like going to her grandma's house because... it was haunted! She just knew the paintings were alive. One day she got kidnapped by one of the soldiers in the painting! He took Aimee to a shack in the linen cupboard and he walked off! She remembered she loved to prank people, so she tied an iron to the handle and it whacked him in the face! She ran to her room. There was a terrible cackle from behind her. Would she survive the night and fall soundly asleep?

Lauren Sibley (8)
Dunstable Icknield Lower School, Dunstable

The Mysterious World

One day the mayonnaise queen was angry, so was everyone in the world, even the witch's magic was out of control. But there was one person that pooped out rainbows! She was made out of a cookie. She wanted to help everyone in the world, so she travelled with some people because she was lonely, and she pooped out the rainbow, and everyone climbed on her. Then they went to the centre because everyone lives there. They made a rainbow and then everyone pooped out rainbows again and they lived happily!

Atrin Amini (8)
Dunstable Icknield Lower School, Dunstable

Minecraft Cake Race

In Wanderberg Kevin and Stampy were having a race to make a cake vs Ibilistic Squid, Nugget and Lee Bear. The ingredients: one egg, two sugar, three buckets of milk and wheat. It had to be made on a crafting table. Milk at the top, egg in the centre, sugar either side, and wheat at the bottom. Stampy and Kevin had a head start because the others were attacked by baby zombies, spiders and creepers! They went to a village got chicken spawns for the eggs and a cow spawn for the milk.They won apparently!

Harry Makinson (8)
Dunstable Icknield Lower School, Dunstable

Daydreaming Day

Exhaustedly, Lucy plopped herself down on the soft sofa. Lazily, she switched on the TV and leant forward. All of a sudden a swirly whirly whirlpool appeared out of nowhere, and sucked Lucy to this pearly land. Confused, she asked, 'Where am I?' to a human next to her.
'Be quiet, King Jeff is coming.'
She bowed down. After, she looked around to find the swirly whirly whirlpool but it disappeared. Obviously she panicked! Then, she heard her teacher say, 'Stop daydreaming and get on with your work!'

Ayaan Chihiro Javid (9)
Forest School, London

The Tornado

Thousands of miles away in Thailand, there was a tornado. There were six brothers and sisters. Jake was the leader. 'Hey guys do you want to... um... go and see the tornado?' Jake scarily offered. They went down to investigate. 'Why don't we go back!' shouted Jake.
Lily, Philip, Poppy, Rosie and Joey were disgusted and replied with a big fat, 'No!'
A huge face appeared. 'Who or what are you,' questioned Lily.
'I'm the demon and I'm here to destroy and take over everything and everywhere!' shouted the demon. Ever since, the children have disappeared.

Safa Islam (9)
Forest School, London

The Real Cinderella Story

I'm sure you know the story about Cinderella but this is what really happened...
One morning, Cinderella was dusting the house when someone knocked on the door, which Cinderella answered. It was the prince! He invited us to his ball and my daughters and Cinderella got our dresses ready. When it was time to leave, my daughter Diana ripped Cinderella's dress! She couldn't go to the ball, so I offered to stay with her. All night Cindy was saying, 'The fairy godmother is going to come and save us...' but she never came!

Robyn Hurwitz (9)
Forest School, London

The Lump Of Doom!

I snatched a lump from my garden. It bit my leg like so. My leg went huge, mushy and bouncy. So I asked the doctor to hack it off. The doctor did what he was told immediately.

The next day I tripped, my other leg fell into the lump. So I chopped it off. I couldn't walk so I had to limp. I slipped and fell, my whole body fell into the lump. I was doomed. How would I do anything? I couldn't move. Well I could move but I had to roll! After a few days I was lumpy...

Isabelle Headlam (8)
Forest School, London

Mountain Girl

There was once a girl called Beatrice. Happily, she lived with her mother and father in a simply enormous mountain.

Tragically, one day her mother and father were eaten by flesh eating wolves. Another day she confidently decided to climb down the mountain to find shelter and food. It took long and horrible hours, but at last, Beatrice reached the bottom. There, she found a home and a family to take her in. She was welcomed into the small village. Eventually she married and lived with her husband for ever and ever. Beatrice lived happily ever after.

Sofia Borrini (9)
Forest School, London

The Dead Of Night

Jacky ran along the dark sidewalk as quick as a cat, dressed in black. No, literally! Jacky was a shapeshifter and could shapeshift into anything. As she ran, she came across a run-down flat. Slowly coming to a halt, Jacky scurried into the nearby alleyway. Looking around her body melted, then suddenly stretched up, revealing a tall slim girl with short, black hair. In a flash she broke down the door, knocked out the guard and shapeshifted into him. Standing by the door she suddenly heard footsteps. She spun round and a dagger plunged ruthlessly into her beating heart.

Zainab Ali (11)
Forest School, London

Pluto Is One Playful Dwarf Planet!

'I'm off to the moon!' I shouted excitedly from my rocket ship. Suddenly there was rattling. The autopilot told me to divert to Pluto. 'Urgh Pluto,' I groaned., I flew to Pluto. As I landed in a rough, bumpy manner, a group of multicoloured dogs that looked like Pluto from Mickey Mouse hit a large button and started partying. It was an 'Earthling Welcome' party. After staring in awe, I joined in. I partied hard for a long time, then I realised that just because Pluto is small, it doesn't mean there isn't a party going on up there.

Keisha Nliam (11)
Forest School, London

Time Travel Maniac

'Jack, look after your sister,' shouted Mum. Mum and Dad were going on a lovey dovey cruise. This time they were going to go to Morocco. So I have to stay with Jack.

From the top of the stairs Jack shouted, 'Josie, help me clean the basement.' The basement was full of rubbish. I found a really weird object. I started fiddling with it. Suddenly me and Jack found ourselves somewhere else. This was the future! We have to find our way home. We found the machine and fiddled with it. We landed back home.

Nironaa Nirmalan (11)
Forest School, London

Tall Tales

'Nooo! You can't!' shouted Mike.

'We can!' replied Mike's mum. They've been trying for months to get Mike to play in a tournament and coaxed him to play.

Mike had the ball at his feet when he was hit by a cyclone of a challenge. 'Aagh! help! He's done me!' screamed Mike.

At the hospital Mike felt nervous. He walked into the X-ray room knowing nothing had happened. Shock spread as the result came. 'How could you?' asked Alice.

'I had to,' Mike mumbled. Mike was never trusted again because of one big lie, he learnt never to lie again.

Qasim Khan (10)
Forest School, London

The Return

Steve Macoy had one dream, to be a footballer. His mum, Joanna, is a widow and is running short on money.
One day they win the lottery, the first thing they do is fly to Florida. It wasn't as perfect as they hoped it would be as Steve loses his left foot in a shark attack. His dream of being a footballer was over, or so he thought. Using the rest of the money they asked Professor Green who makes fake body parts, to help.
Nine years later he's playing for England and is the best footballer in the world.

Finlay Forbes Cooper (10)
Forest School, London

Unlucky Times Pay Off

The beautiful sunrise was sitting on the water. Tim Shiver zoomed around on his new boat. After this, assuming Captain Cutless' boat was his dad's, he clambered aboard to find pirates surrounding him. With sweat trickling down his spine, he attempted to barge his way through the muscular men, but sadly failed.
After weeks of his stay, his shipmates questioned if Tim could be adviser, as he was so smart. Cutless agreed with this. Shortly after this decision, they faced a storm. Everyone was wiped out. Washed ashore, on a sandy beach the colour of the sun, they settled happily.

Finn Sweetnam (10)
Forest School, London

Untitled

Sam Green was a happy man. He had just won £30,000 from the casino. A Burger King was 50 metres away and he decided to get a cheeseburger, he had money to burn now. Walking in he noticed that there were no people in the Burger King. If he was feeling alert then he may have noticed that it was not a Burger King, in fact it was a poison store, home to the most deadly poison in the world. Sam Green ordered his burger and ate for about ten minutes. When finished, he sat back and his breathing failed.

Angus Horn (10)
Forest School, London

The Lonely Mermaid

Once upon a time there was a lonely mermaid whose only friend was a fish called Simon.
One day the mermaid and Simon saw a human on the seashore. The mermaid and Simon wanted to be friends with the human. The mermaid came over to her and said hello.
They all became friends.
The human girl was called Jenny.
Jenny gave the mermaid a name that reminded her of the sea: Coral. Coral gave Jenny magic powers so she could swim and breathe underwater.
They all swam and played together. Coral, Simon and Jenny became best friends for ever!

Amber Butt (7)
Forest School, London

The Talking Cat

Just as my owners (Oscar and Stella) left I did my morning stretches and went to eat my food (Whiskas meat in jelly cat food). Once I had finished, I considered having a nap on the roof, those tiles warm up incredibly quickly, you know. But no, instead I decided to go to the Alley Restaurant. They serve the best mouse and rat cuisine on the block. That done I went back home where I got into a row with Max the mouse. My owners came back as I shouted, 'Go away!' at Max.
'You can speak?'
'Yes, I can...'

Oscar Bob Weaver Marder (10)
Forest School, London

The Great Big Bang

The explosion sent a supersonic boom across the sky of Planet Earth. It was chaos. The whole world had a tantrum. Inside Russia's NASA space laboratory, Dr Zack was constantly typing away, confused of what occurred. This was out of date from the space calendar. The Earth rumbled causing Dr Zack to collapse into unconsciousness.
Four hours later he rose from his sleep and went to consult his colleagues, all of them hairy, crouching on the floor, devouring bananas! He went to the bathroom to clear his vision, however he appeared completely ordinary in the mirror. He was doomed.

Ruhaab Amir (10)
Forest School, London

The Phoenix

Ben went to the forest to find a phoenix, Ben wanted to see if the rumours were true. He searched many times before, but he failed. Today he was going to work for hours. Ben thought to himself, *the things people say probably aren't true!* Suddenly, he heard the cry of a phoenix. The noise echoed through the forest. He knew immediately he was close. Ben took out his machete and sliced the leaves with the greatest of ease. A flame shot out above the trees. These hours paid off! His dream came true. Today was the best day ever!

Ranveer Marway (10)
Forest School, London

Tim And The Dodos

Tim was going on a school trip when he fell into a strange portal that led into space. He shouted, 'Can you hear me?' As he didn't know he was in outer space. When he did find out, it was only then he thought, *how am I breathing? And I'm heading to Jupiter.* As he flashed into Jupiter, he began to see little creatures like birds on Jupiter.
When he got down, there was a dodo that said, 'A human, guards get him!' Then, suddenly, Tim turned green then brown, then he shrunk, shrunk and shrunk. Tim the Dodo Man!

Albert Ainger (8)
Forest School, London

The Alien's Friend

Mike was travelling to Earth. He was very excited because he was going to make a friend. Suddenly he asked his mum, 'How long till we're there?'
Then his mum replied, 'In one hour and twenty minutes.'
Once they had landed, Mike immediately ran out of the spaceship and towards London, so his mum shouted, 'Wait for me!'. As the clocks struck eight o'clock Mike and his mum were snoring in a hotel in the middle of London.
That Monday Mike met a boy named Harry and made good friends with him.
That night his mum said, 'We are staying!'

Harry Joyce (8)
Forest School, London

Jack Meets Dragons

Jack and his friend Harry are running in a huge jungle where you can find all sorts of creatures. While they were running they saw two dragons flying in the air on the look-out for anyone that doesn't belong in the jungle. The dragons' names were Max and Finley. Then they saw Jack and Harry. 'Look!' shouted Max, 'there are some little children.' Then suddenly Jack and Harry saw the dragons coming to them, they ran for their lives. 'Never come back!' said Max.
'We won't,' said Jack, and they ran back home.

Charley Kernon (7)
Forest School, London

The Alien Who Found A Friend

Once there was a snake in a huge jungle. One day the snake heard a *bang!* Then he saw a weird-looking aircraft. The snake slithered to the aircraft and saw a big hole in the ground. Suddenly the snake heard a loud voice and saw a green, sloppy person. The snake said, 'Who are you?'
'I am an alien!'
'I came here to look for a friend!'
'Can you be my friend?'
'Yes!' said the snake.
They found the hole and they got the rocks and parts of the Earth and decided to repair the ground.

Jeevan Singh Kathuria (8)
Forest School, London

Elemental Planets

Jeff, Jack, Henry and Darwin were sleeping. One day when Jeff woke up, Jeff and his friends had been teleported to a different galaxy. There were so many planets to explore. So he and his friends went to the fire planet and learnt some awesome fire moves. Next they went to the ice planet and learnt snow spiryitsu. After that, they went to an electricity planet, and learnt epic thunder spells.Then, they went to a water planet and learnt to swim swiftly. Finally they went back to Earth and had a massive dinner together at a restaurant.

Khalil Kayani (8)
Forest School, London

The Endangered Life

One day Ben and Sophie were out on a picnic. Ben felt something. The floor got smaller and they disappeared, but nobody knew where they went. A scientist discovered that Ben went to the past and Sophie went to the future. There was only one way to get out – a magic portal you had to go in and it would take you anywhere you want. Literally anywhere. Ben met some Vikings and some Romans, but Sophie met some ballerinas and they both met and celebrated, but had to clean up very, very unfair!

Qaim Shah (7)
Forest School, London

Apocalypse

I heard a sound, a terrifying sound. I peered out the window, blazing fire covering the city! *Knock...* I quickly ran downstairs, and locked the door. Right at that moment a sniper shot me in the hand! 'Arrr!' I ran towards the sniper, dodging the shots. I shut the window, I ran up the stairs into my bathroom turning the tap on trying to get the bullet out. I could hear them screaming, 'This is the time to fight!' I get my rifle, *bang!* It still works. I opened the window, this is it, the end. *Bang, bang, bang...*

Nathan Wright (9)
Forest School, London

The Bottomless Pit

Larry was jumping about in the park. Dave arrived afterwards, and dared Larry to jump over the bottomless pit. Larry started to jump and suddenly saw something swaying down below. He quickly hung onto the edge. He was just in time. One more second and he'd be gobbled. The figure was a dragon. They decided to electrocute it so it would fall and it worked! Finally, Larry was able to attempt his dare... but he ended up in the bottomless pit.

Rafi Uddin Khan (9)
Forest School, London

Suddenly...

The scorching heat was melting my face. Suddenly I heard a growling roar behind me which was ear-splittingly loud. My hand was shaking with fear, then out of nowhere a huge, crimson dragon erupted from the ground, sending sand and rocks flying up into the dark sky above. I held my breath and angrily attempted to slice off the monstrous beast's head. I closed my eyes, hoping to hear the loud cry of it falling to the ground. There it was, I watched as the dragon fell, The ground shook. I heard low grumbles from somewhere; dragon's grumbles?

Finlay Kinnaird (9)
Forest School, London

The Minions In Star Wars

In a far-off land there once lived three minions, Bob, Stuart and Dave. They got blasted into a different galaxy and found Star Wars. The Jedi were amazing, the minions helped defeat foes and were rewarded with glinting gold medals with a red strap. Sadly, in the space of one day, the Sith had taken the power of the Galactic Empire. Luckily, the minions were there to save the day! Amazingly the minions got given the crystal glasses of honour.

Luke Miller (9)
Forest School, London

Allen The Alien

Allen the alien was going to get his usual breakfast when suddenly a glint of light caught his eye. Quickly, he hopped into his spaceship to get a better look at this mysterious light. He got up close and realised it was a new planet. Quickly he checked on his computer to make sure the air was OK to breathe in. It was fine. He stepped out of his spaceship, when suddenly he saw an animal. He didn't know what kind it was but it looked perilous, it quickly sprinted out of sight. He wondered what other surprises this planet would bring...

Peter Miller (9)
Forest School, London

The Last Bullet

A man strolled into Tim's detective agency, then he spoke, 'My friend's been... murdered!' I finally found the dark street his neighbours lived on, I heard two screams and two men fell from a window. I recognised them. A neighbour.

A minute later, a man with beady eyes stepped out of the house. He pelted forward to a man. 'Where's the money?' The other man handed him a pale envelope. I followed him to a mansion. He went in and I followed intrepidly. He saw me, I pulled out my pistol, fired. After a minute I fired my last bullet...

Óran Donal Docker (9)
Forest School, London

The Eagle Wolves

Clambering up the steep, rocky mountain I sensed I was close. My quest is to find the deadly tooth of an eagle wolf. Then I saw it, the cave of the eagle wolves. My heart was pounding, my legs quivering. Slowly I tiptoed towards the mouth of the cave, then entered. It stank! I approached the biggest sleeping wolf, then as it opened its giant mouth, *yank!* the tooth came out easily then... the wolf suddenly awoke! I ran towards the cave entrance and hid in a small hole. Would the wolves miss me or would they find me?

Miles Whitchelo (9)
Forest School, London

My Adventures In The Land Of Minecraftia

Zap! Where am I and why is everything cube? Oh my gosh! Am I in the world of Minecraftia? Just look at the swaying trees and the serene ocean! *Whoosh!* What was that? Could it be the ferocious, frantic, dangerous, deadly Herobrine? 'Come out, come out wherever you are,' spoke a spooky voice. Then out of nowhere a mythical creature jumped out at me and looked at me in the eye. Then the mythical creature spoke again. 'The fight is just beginning...'

James Brooks (9)
Forest School, London

Gorilla Tale

In the centre of South Africa, a professor was looking for a white gorilla. Finally he found one.
Hours later, he was on the news that night. 'White gorilla has been found!' said the news lady. But what they didn't know was that a common, devious criminal was watching. Green pound signs came out of his red eyes, he knew it was worth money.
The next day he spotted the gorilla and followed him. Luckily security spotted him break through and prison was his reward. The professor decided that he should take the gorilla home. But the gorilla has returned...

Lucas Holland (8)
Forest School, London

Untitled

Suddenly, it swooped down and picked me up. 'Argh!' I screamed in a mournful voice. I couldn't believe it! I was amazed, I was travelling through time!
Suddenly, it came to an end. '10, 9, 8, 7, 6, 5, 4, 3, 2,1 and lift-off,' a man's voice boomed. Wow! It's the Russian aircraft.
Suddenly, four men grabbed me and threw me into the aircraft and I got lifted into space.
'Argh!'
About an hour later, we landed on a planet. I turned into an alien, then I very sadly exploded. *Boom!*

Rayyan Javaid (9)
Forest School, London

The Deadly Truth

Zoe wandered through the lonely graveyard. In front of her were two freshly-dug graves for her mother and father. Behind the graves was a body. Her aunt. Her hand clasped a knife that had been plunged into her heart. In her hand was a note. 'Dear Zoe I am going to tell you the truth. Before your parents died, I owed people money. My boyfriend kept taking mine. I killed your parents so I could inherit their money. I couldn't live with the guilt'.
Zoe stood in a shocked silence. Then she walked away without looking back.

Ria Sukhija (11)
Forest School, London

The Jungle Ruler

Once upon a time there lived a monkey and a tiger. The monkey's name was Cheeky and the tiger's name was Roar. They were sometimes nice and sometimes mean to each other. However, there was one main thing they both wanted, it was to rule the jungle, but they didn't want to rule it together. So Roar and Cheeky kept on fighting until one day the monkey said that they would have half and half, but the tiger didn't agree. He wanted it all for himself. The tiger went to the monkey's house and ate the brown monkey!

Sanaa Shakoor (7)
Forest School, London

How Zoey And Lola Became Friends

There is a girl called Zoey and a girl called Lola. Lola and Zoey were enemies.
One day they had a fight because Zoey and Lola both went to karate and Zoey knocked out Lola! Nobody ever knocked out Lola. So Lola started being unkind to Zoey.
Once they had another fight and Lola fell over and banged her head. Lola needed to go to hospital. It might be bad for Lola but Zoey got her black belt in karate. Zoey went to visit Lola in the hospital. When Lola was out of the hospital, Zoey and Lola became friends.

Abigail Joseph
Forest School, London

Tooth

Once upon a time there was a boy called Ben who lived with his mother. Ben had a wobbly tooth. One night Ben's tooth fell out. He was very happy. On that night he put his tooth under his pillow.
The next morning arrived, he looked under his pillow, all there was, was his tooth.
The next night, he put his tooth under his pillow and fell into a deep sleep. At exactly midnight, the tooth fairy appeared. She got Ben's tooth and replaced it with a £2 coin.
The next morning Ben found his shiny golden £2 coin. Yay!

Amuruthaa Surenkumar (8)
Forest School, London

Luke And The Old Lady

One day Luke went out to buy some peas. When he reached home he planted them.
Next morning Luke woke up and saw that the peas had grown higher than the clouds. Luke climbed the peas and in the clouds he found a cottage. He knocked on the door and an old lady came out and chased Luke down the peas. When Luke reached the bottom he ran into his house and closed the door. Then after a long time a thunderstorm came and the lady was climbing the peas when lightning hit the peas and the lady died!

Radhika Saha (8)
Forest School, London

The Giraffe And The Monkey

Isla, Tom, Kate and Dan were going to an island. It took them an hour to get there. When they got there, it was peace. All they found was one emerald, one amber, two rubies and three diamonds. Then they found a monkey called Swing and a giraffe called Zous. They were best friends. They were looking for gems. As soon as they told them they were so happy. They told them every gem grants 65 wishes. After that they were so happy living on an island. They became best friends for ever. They loved it, it was amazing there.

Leianna Espinosa (7)
Forest School, London

The Evil Clown, Badger And The Porcupine

One day a clown was trying to kidnap a badger, so it could be his pet but the gallant porcupine saved him. The porcupine and the badger started to spend more time together. The badger grew fond of the porcupine, but evil was keeping them apart, so the badger asked if they could go for a walk in the forest looking for evil, but actually at the end of the forest there was a table with a candle and two plates. The porcupine said yes, but he didn't know what was in store for him. Badger had made a potion...

Anna Christine Biles (8)
Forest School, London

How Tom Met Lucy

There was a girl called Lucy who lived with her poor parents. One day the parents couldn't feed themselves, so they kicked Lucy out! While Lucy begged for food she met a man who pushed her over into the mud.

Suddenly a boy came along and said, 'I'm Tom, come to my house so we can get you clean.' Lucy slowly walked to Tom's house. When she got there she said, 'I don't care about getting clean but please let me live here, I can do housework.' So Tom agreed and all of them lived happily ever after. Yay!

Amber Sienna Jain (8)
Forest School, London

Fairies To The Rescue

Once upon a time, there lived seven fairies who are friends called Abigail, Emma, Anna, Grace, Amber, Amy and Nicole. They all lived in a tree in a park.

One day Billy the giant accidentally fell off his cloud and tumbled all the way down to Earth. He was very angry, and he had a branch stuck in his foot. It was so funny because he landed in the park where the fairies lived. The fairies were picking strawberries. Suddenly, a thud made the Earth shake. Then the fairies crept and saw Billy crying, so they went to help him.

Damara Williams (8)
Forest School, London

The Monkey Escape

One day Emily, Joe, Elaine and Patrick went to see the monkeys. As soon as they had their tickets they went to see the screeching monkeys. The sign said there were meant to be seven monkeys but there was only six. Joe found the monkey enclosure door open for some reason. Joe told Emily to shut the gate so no more monkeys could escape. Emily spotted the monkey that had escaped, ran to catch up with him, but he was too fast. They saw the monkey run out of the big gates. They saw the monkey on the dusty road....

Emma Kelsey (8)
Forest School, London

The Tooth Fairy Adventure

A little girl was asleep in her bed and she had lost a tooth and it was under her pillow. The tooth fairy was at the end of the little girl's bed waiting for the right time to sneak and get the tooth. When the fairy did it the girl felt something and woke up. The girl saw the fairy and they decided to be friends. The fairy made the little girl fairy-sized and gave her wings. They both flew off to collect teeth. They were both very happy because they were best friends. They had a bag full.

Amy Rose Manning (8)
Forest School, London

Aliens Ate Me For Dinner!

I stopped, dismounted my bike and watched as a bright green light sped towards me. As it got closer I started to panic. My heart sped up. Then all of a sudden I felt an uplifting feeling through my body as if I was flying. When I opened my eyes I was inside some sort of UFO. I tried to stand up. I was tied down. As strange, mysterious creatures crowded around me, my heart started skipping beats. I was forced into saying my last words. 'Please don't eat me,' I murmured. Then they all fed on my flesh.

Krishan Arawwawala (11)
Forest School, London

The Chance

Jack loves to play football and longs to play for a club, but his mum doesn't have enough money and already knows he has what it takes.
One day when he was playing in his local park, a tall figure emerged. Jack froze as he saw the person. 'Who are you?' exclaimed Jack.
'Calm down kid, I'm a scout and I've just been watching, you're good, very good. I want to sign you up to Leyton Orient and I'm guessing you don't have enough money looking at your boots, the choice is yours kid.'

Temilade Kogbe (11)
Forest School, London

The Chest

Sarah sat on the faded leather armchair, her gaze fixed to the bright screen of her phone. 'Die you pig!' Sarah yelled.
'What's wrong? Boyfriend dump you?' asked Sophie, whilst reading.
'Ha, ha, very funny. I'm playing Angry Birds,' replied Sarah.
'I'm so bored,' Sophie mumbled leaning against the bookshelf. Suddenly the bookshelf opened with a click.
'Wow does your grandad know this is here?' asked Sarah pocketing her phone.
'Er no,' Sophie replied. There was a chest in the middle of the room. As soon as they saw it they opened it, there was a flash and then silence...

William Headlam (11)
Forest School, London

The Slow Duck

At the start of the race it was silent. 3, 2, 1, go! The snail and the duck ran and ran but the duck was not in the lead! The snail was. The duck was trying and trying but still not in the lead. In the end the snail had a nap, but the duck still did not win. Then he had an idea, he would make himself be sick, so he had an excuse that he did not win the race...

George Newland (11)
Forest School, London

The Mugging

It was just another ordinary day for Tom. Or so he thought. But little did he know that around this corner were three muggers. As Tom turned the corner they pounced, momentarily paralysing him. He heard someone scream then some sirens but saw nothing. He tried to fight but was easily overpowered by the three bandits. Yelling did nothing as his voice was muffled and silent. Sirens sounded all around him but they were still quite distant. They finally got closer but he feared it was too late. Was this the end or would he make it through?

Josua Eric Biles (11)
Forest School, London

School

Just finishing the register there was a crash and a boom sound. I went to go and check it out and there standing right in front of me was Bob the Villain.
'He's here!' exclaimed Madam Mahum.
'Who?' asked Alice the Alien.
'Bob the Villain!'
'Let out the gadgets and destroy him!'
They all rushed to help. There was silence.
'We saved everyone. Yay!' Alice the Alien screeched.
All of the Martians came out of their hiding places and they all celebrated!
'Oh, I just realised it was a fake fire alarm!'

Mahum Farooq (9)
Forest School, London

Tower Of Terror

Lost! Charlie stood shivering with fear. He had no clue where he was in the ancient Tower of London. Every turn he made was the wrong turn. All of a sudden he heard footsteps following him. Charlie could hear footsteps getting closer and closer and closer! He stood still and closed his eyes. His heart was beating so fast, sweat was dripping from his head. Then suddenly something grabbed his shoulder! It was a security guard coming to take him back home. All he wanted to do was go home and relax whilst watching TV. Home sweet home.

Molly Rees (10)
Forest School, London

Dangerous World

As I stepped out the door, wind brushed against my face. I've heard rumours about this place. I approached my affable friends but the sight they can't bear. They've left in disgust. I trembled through the forest, it begins to grow darker. The screeching as the owls fly past me. I walked closer, and to my eyes there it was. As curiosity took over me, I advanced closer and closer. I could not believe it... it couldn't be. The figure left me abandoned on the banks of the stream. I've seen him before. Who is this dark figured person?

Anya Patel (10)
Forest School, London

The Lonely Woods

Breathless, I rested against the large oak tree. My ankles screamed of agony since I'd been on the run for hours. Suddenly I heard pounding footsteps. 'Alex, where are you sweetheart?' the sing-song voice shouted.

My heart pounded against my chest. My mind was saying to climb the tree but my heart was telling me to run. I started to climb the tree as big as a giant. No one dared to come into the lonely woods since everyone had their tales. Leaves covered me and there was a bang! The soft wind was left...

Ananya Lal (10)
Forest School, London

Apples

Pluck, Clare pulled an apple off a ripe, juicy tree. A lace shadow carpeted the floor. Clare heard something creep towards her. She thought nothing of it and tore a large chunk out of the apple. *Crunch!* She heard it again but this time the leaves rustled like a hurricane. Sweat beads gripped her face. The crunching noise was like crumbling bones. All her thoughts spun like a tornado in her head. Regret filled her eyes, sweat trickled down onto the ground... she then realise it was only a curious horse looking for food. Giving him the apples, Clare ran off.

Viola Neuls Humphreys (10)
Forest School, London

Gone Wild

Slam! Jambo (an elephant is getting knocked out). *Bam!* Jambo fell to the ground. Jambo's eyes started to close. Mysteriously a monkey popped up in front of Jambo. It gasped, 'Hi, I'm Ballo and you are?'
'I'm Jambo.'
Ballo spoke, 'Come with me.' Ballo led Jambo into the jungle. When Ballo touched a giant vine Jambo started to shiver. Ballo exclaimed, 'Come on it's not scary at all.'
As soon as Jambo got on the vine he crashed into a huge rock attached to a cliff. Suddenly Jambo woke up in his really cosy bed.

India Shepperson (11)
Forest School, London

A Tragic Story

Amy stepped onto the gleaming red gondola, her heavy boots weighing her down. She was all alone. This is how her story began. She was halfway up the ski lift when suddenly the gondola started shaking. She felt the floor trembling beneath her feet. Her heart was pounding like a mighty drum. Sweat was rolling down her face and onto the floor. Then it happened. The whole world turned to darkness. Amy felt cold, wet, unknown and since then no one has used that gondola and no one has found little Amy Salavon.

Holly Gibson
Forest School, London

The Birthday Party

It was Laila's first ever birthday party. She was very nervous, but also excited. She arrived and saw everyone from her class was there. While everyone was playing, from a distance Laila saw a rabbit. She followed it to the garden. 'Say these words: happy, happy, happy and you will be a rabbit too!' said the bunny. 'And also can you save my brother?' So they set off. When they came back Laila hopped into the house only to see that the party was finished and Ellie was handing out party bags which had a cute pink rabbit inside.

Aliye Sevim Aktas (9)
Forest School, London

Spies Undercover

Another horrific day again. Lizzie got bullied. She paced herself back home because a strange person was following her. Lizzie knew this person so she stopped. Phew, it was her spy partner Milly.
Bob, their spy leader said, 'After school, villains are trying to kill the queen. You have to stop them.'
Quickly they ran up the hundreds of steps. They snuck up behind the villains and tackled them.
'Oh deary me. Thank you girls,' said the glorious queen. The queen gave Lizzie and Milly pure gold crowns. When they came back to their village they were heroes.

Kate Dempsey (11)
Forest School, London

The Alleyway

Felicity dragged herself down the pitch-black, gloomy alleyway. She heard footsteps echoing in the distance. She could feel her heart pounding in her chest while sweat trickled down her pale forehead. At the corner of her eye she caught a glimpse of a towering shadow. An enormous hand reached out and grabbed Felicity. She shrieked with horror. 'Please do not worry. I'm not trying to hurt you. I'm just here to return this KitKat you dropped!' The man reassured her and with that Felicity ran home and never went down any alleyways ever again.

Amelia Deery (10)
Forest School, London

A Walk To School

My eyes sagged with exhaustion. I could barely keep them open. I thought I would collapse. I did. My eyes just managed to open. Darkness was in my presence. All I remember was a walk to school. Where was I? I tried to get up, the ground was pulling me down. Now I know how it feels to be rope in tug-of-war. As I caught a glimpse of the creature, my heart beat fast. My brain ordered me to wake it up. Before I could do it, the creature jumped off a cliff. This story is a cliff-hanger.

Hana Azeem (9)
Forest School, London

The Lonely Child

It was dark but I wasn't afraid. I tiptoed down the stairs and sneaked out of the orphanage door. I was free. I just needed some money so I decided to be a pickpocket. I was stealing for three days and got £100. I spent it on clothes and food. It was the best day of my life until I saw a girl. She was homeless and hopeless. I walked up to her and gave her some bread. I gave her a coat. Suddenly I had an idea. I took her and I to a lovely caring orphanage.

Ellie Joyce (10)
Forest School, London

Winter's Breath Creatures

I ran outside. This is what I had been waiting for all year round. The first torrent of snow. There was no time to waste. As I excitedly bounded into the mound of soft, crumbly snow, I let out a satisfied sigh. My breath was a cascade of fine mist. Even as I was looking, it changed into a dragon and a knight fighting an underwater creature. All around me, children were playing in the snow blanketed on my home town. I realised I didn't want to join them. I was happy here, playing with my winter's breath creatures.

Marnie McPartland (9)
Forest School, London

What Have You Done?

'No!' Sophie yelled. Her heart was falling to pieces. Jumping on her horse she rode away, sobbing blindly into Scarlet's thick mane with her vibrant red hair flying behind her. Her mother had destroyed her. Killed the only thing that made her live. Her bow. The whistle of it in the air. She loved it. She slowed the horse down to a trot. Sophie thought to herself; suddenly she realised her mother just wanted her to be happy. 'What have I done?' muttered Sophie, racing back on her horse to see her mother.
'Darling', cried her mum, 'I'm so sorry!'

Tabitha Galliers (10)
Forest School, London

Trombone Trouble

Screech! Lucy put her trombone down in anguish. Her usually-blue eyes were grey. The wretched instrument hadn't been working for ages. Shoulders sagging, Lucy trudged home in great despair feeling around for the hanky which was the family heirloom. Lucy couldn't find it.
'Charlie!' she called, 'the hanky's gone.'
Charlie bounded upstairs in aid of her sister.
'My trombone doesn't work, I've lost the hanky,' Lucy cried.
Charlie picked up the trombone and played. It didn't work. She put her hand through the hole feeling the hanky. Lucy was overjoyed at the news. They didn't speak of it again.

Ameya Ramani (10)
Forest School, London

The Candy-Eating Giant

Suddenly out of nowhere came the giant. Giant Sara! She started eating everything. The candyfloss clouds, the candy cane trees and the lollipop people. Lolmon, Loliloopsy and Loopyloop had to do something about it. (They were all lollipop people.) After long and painful hours they tied Sara up with giant liquorice ropes! They were heroes and were admired for generations. While everyone was parading, Sara was locked up in the sticky caramel dungeon. She escaped by eating her way out, and then she took the waffle, syrupy strawberries and cream rocket home. Sara was thankfully never, ever seen again.

Sara Khan (9)
Forest School, London

Chaos At School

Bursting into tears, I strolled into school. How embarrassing it was when I trotted through the wretched gates. As I sat on my chair, everyone was glaring their eyes at me. Butterflies fluttering in my stomach. My taunting teacher telling me to finish my frustrating work. Everyone was giggling at me. My devastating dragon head teacher was where I was going to get sent to next. Piled on my desk were books of unfinished work. Quietly, I tried to tiptoe out of my chair and escape from the school. I wondered where I'd be sent to next...

Lara Khambh (9)
Forest School, London

Too Fast

I was running along the platform laughing as my best friend bumped into me. I tripped and fell. I fell like it was slow motion. I hit the floor. The train was too fast for me. I didn't even realise it was over me. It was too fast. Too fast for me to realise I was gone. No time to say goodbye. Nobody knows where I have gone. I wasn't ready to go. I still had my life to live.

Lily St.Ville (11)
Forest School, London

Aliens In Space!

Onboard the spaceship was the amazing team of Stella, Louise and Martin. Their ship was malfunctioning. 'I'll go down to the control room to see what's wrong,' called Martin.
After he left there were thuds and a scream. In the steering room, Louise and Stella looked alarmed at each other.
'I'll go and see what's wrong,' Louise explained. Not long after she'd gone there was a piercing scream. Cautiously, Stella peered in, a grotesque creature looked back. She ran to the escape craft. As she blasted to space she saw the ship covered with them. What would happen now?

Mysha Ali (11)
Forest School, London

The Girl Who Got Turned Into Pasta

Lucy was a monster when it came to dinner time. Every time her mother cooked her something she would chuck it on the floor! One day her mother went off shopping, consequently Lucy was left all alone in the house. She sprinted off to get ready for bed. Suddenly she heard the door open. She thought it was her mum and was ready to throw a tantrum. However, it was the Spaghetti Man! Instantly Lucy found herself in the pasta factory. She tried to escape but she was rapidly formed into lasagne! So watch out kiddos!

Iman Monir (10)
Forest School, London

The Magic Cupboard

Bursting for the potion, Charlie raced to the cupboard. Suddenly, the door banged shut. 'Oi! Help me get out of this wretched cupboard!' yelled Charlie. He felt as if he was falling down a deep hole. He opened his eyes, he was in the future and a titanic, hairy creature grabbed him and took him to a giant spaceship. He fell into a box that was as dark as the night.
'Who is this?' a voice boomed.
'Need him to help us,' someone shivered.
Charlie was gone. He arrived at the cupboard.
'Where are you Charlie?' yelled the teacher.

Juliet Wong (9)
Forest School, London

The Demon Headmaster

'The Forest School grub shop was full of giggling boys stuffing their mouths with sweets washed down with Cola. Suddenly the outline of a man became clearer. His eyes were like twin orbs of hell fire. Then he stretched out one withered finger. At first no one noticed then there was a shriek. The boys headed out like buffalo.' Grandpa paused before continuing. 'Out of the polar-white clouds dropped a bomb whistling a tune of death as it fell. The explosion was spectacular. The headmaster was an angel not a demon that saved them (including me).' Grandpa finished. 'Bedtime!'

Ria Roy (8)
Forest School, London

Mermaid's Treasure

In the depths of the ocean, Maria the mermaid swiftly glided through the serene ocean like a hawk.
There he was: Tritanus the guard of the pearl of the depth. 'O Maria, how do we pass him?' whispered Goldy the fish.
'Watch this,' replied Maria. With her powers, she blasted Tritanus with a sudden blast of blinding light. He was knocked out. As she swam, vicious vines reached for her and grabbed her and she could not break free. Fortunately, Goldy could break free and he snapped the vines with his sharp teeth. Swimming really quickly, Maria grabbed the beautiful pearl.

Jamila Mohamudbucus (8)
Forest School, London

Time Machine

Ella made a huge time travelling machine which worked so she got in and *whoosh* – she flew faster and faster into the future. In the future she met a man called Zork. Because she was new she got a special robot alien called Bob. Bob showed her around all the cool technology, like a cool computer that prints anything 3D. It was also edible. There was also an amazing invisibility cloak. The best one is the weather machine.
She said, 'This is all nice but I want to go home!'
Suddenly her daddy shouted, 'Time to wake up!'

Athene Macnamara (8)
Forest School, London

A Day At The Beach

Looking around and taking in the scene. I saw the rotating, aquamarine sea, the little children swarming around me and the yellow sand. I could feel the soft golden sand. Taking a deep breath through my nose I could smell the ice cream and hot dogs making me ravenous. I could hear the white horses crashing into the beach and the oldies screaming at the children to come back. It was a glorious day. Being here made me happy. Being here made bubbles of excitement flow in my stomach.

Kaitlin Lovell (9)
Forest School, London

The Portal Of Doom

The jungle hunter found a spiral type of portal, he went in. It said: 'Portal of Doom Entrance.' He landed in the Jungle of Doom. He took out his diamond spear, waiting for something to come out of the bushes. A tiger about twenty metres in length pounced on the jungle hunter. The jungle hunter drove his spear right through the jungle tiger's heart. Suddenly the tiger came back alive and pounced on the jungle hunter's face and ripped it to pieces. The jungle hunter was no more. The tiger went around the area for more intruders.

Amar Bhangu (8)
Forest School, London

Starfight Guns And Asteroids

On the misty planet Max and Syrus climbed onto land. Syrus and Max were gripped with excitement. Max saw an alien and got his space taser out. The alien dived into the hole just in time. Max and Syrus shot down the hole with jetpacks. Max tasered the alien and lasered a hole. They crept through a shaft and into a pod. They drove into an alien city. They got out the grenades that make aliens sleep. They retrieved gold. They got into the master pod. They got back to Earth safely.

Syrus Azonwanna-Pratt
Forest School, London

The Lizard Who Lost His Tail

Once there was a lizard. He was getting chased by a hunter. The hunter cut off the lizard's tail. The lizard was screaming in pain as he ran far away from the hunter. When the lizard stopped he fainted. When the lizard woke up he searched far and wide but he couldn't find it anywhere. He went back to the hunter but he saw a tiger. The tiger was attacking the hunter so he quickly ran in and distracted the hunter while the tiger was attacking. He ran back and slept. When he woke up he had a tail.

Malakai Foster (7)
Forest School, London

Wicked Cinderella And Her Lonely Family

Wicked Cinderella lives with her lovely family. She treats them like slaves while she lives a luxurious life. News came that the prince was throwing a ball to choose his new, beautiful wife. Gracefully Cinderella and the prince danced around. However, when Cinderella left she left her handbag. The prince picked it up. Sneakily he looked inside to find a plan that said that Cinderella wanted to steal the prince's money.
Finally, he marries Anastasia and lives happily ever after. Although, Drizzella wanted to marry the prince so she plotted a plan to marry him... This is the actual story.

Tanisha Sen (9)
Forest School, London

The Girl And The Pegasus

Once upon a time there was a girl called Ruby; her favourite thing to do was horse riding. One day Ruby found a magical stream, which, if you jumped in, you would get teleported to a magical forest. So Ruby jumped in. When Ruby was in the forest she met a pink Pegasus. The Pegasus was tied up so Ruby helped the Pegasus. When the Pegasus was free, it asked if she wanted a ride. Ruby rode it and it took her to a magical kingdom filled with Pegasuses. All the Pegasuses were happy to see the other Pegasus.

Chloe Roberts
Frieth CEC School, Henley-On-Thames

The Workhouse Rules

Amanda was a workhouse girl who was unlike all the other girls, brave. She stood up for what she thought was right and didn't like being told what to do. One day the girls were trudging down for their revolting meal when Amanda saw someone being flogged. She felt sympathetic for her so she grabbed hold of the whip. The furious mistress whipped Amanda so hard the cane almost broke. However Amanda was cunning. She and the girls refused to work until they were told that beating was banned. The enraged mistress had no choice but to fulfil their wish.

Emma Sage (10)
Frieth CEC School, Henley-On-Thames

The Not Very Brave Sea Turtle

Once there was a sea turtle. His name was Ranny. He was not very brave at all. He lived in a very busy town named Coral Reef. But one night when everyone was sleeping a big shark came and took everyone but not Ranny. He looked out of his window and everyone had gone. He said to himself, 'I've got to get them.' So he did. Ranny searched far away but no sign of them. Then he heard some shouting. He saw them all in a cage. He quickly opened the cage and freed them and Ranny was a hero.

Ava Mae Ainsworth (9)
Frieth CEC School, Henley-On-Thames

Dear Diary

Dear Diary, my name is Victoria, you can call me Vic. I died in 1901. Now it's time to play. My husband died. Soldiers came into our house and said we were going to have a photo taken. Everyone wore their favourite clothes and jewellery. They even carried their dogs. We were all ready. Suddenly soldiers came in with guns and shot everyone. I was so sad I wore black for the rest of my life. Sadly I got killed too. So here I am writing in my diary. I am a ghost writing in my diary; ready to haunt people.

Scarlett May Courtney (10)
Frieth CEC School, Henley-On-Thames

Toothend

Once upon a time Princess Sparkle lived at Toothend Village. As night fell an evil mastermind without the permission of Princess Sparkle, Fang – the most threatening, evil fairy living, arrived wearing a black cloak and wings, with a hammer in one hand. *Tap-tap.* Tired, Princess Sparkle heard a noise. *'Ha-ha!'* She knew that laugh... it was Fang.
She sent for her guards to capture Fang. They rode out on bumblebees and swooped up behind him. He was captured! All the tooth fairies happily cheered, but Fang sat in the corner and cried.

Ruby Marshall (9)
Frieth CEC School, Henley-On-Thames

A Bad, Turning Into
A Worse, Dream

Dear Diary, today I had an amazing dream. I dreamt that my dog , Rex, and I had discovered a mystical island that had living dinosaurs on it. There were T-rexes and diplodocus and even triceratops. Oh, and I was also in the middle of a verdant, shimmering jungle with trees the size of skyscrapers, and leaves the size of tables. It was fascinating but scary at the same time. Do I go left? Do I go right? I can't tell! Everything looks the same. I want my mummy. I'm home... Wait, that wasn't a dream. I'm stranded on an island.

Sam Warnes (10)
Frieth CEC School, Henley-On-Thames

Wives

Henry VIII was a greedy, stubborn man who had no respect for others. Unkind though he was, Henry wanted a son. He found the only way to get one would be to get married. Henry married soon after the decision but this wife wasn't for him so eventually they divorced. Even if it didn't work out first time, Henry was so eager for a son he remarried another woman. But there was only one lady out there for him. He just hadn't found her yet. So three wives went by and finally he found the one. The perfect couple (nearly!).

Jessie Harper (9)
Frieth CEC School, Henley-On-Thames

The Necklace

Hello I'm Carell, I live under the sea. I'm a mermaid. Last week I was swimming past a deep hole when suddenly my necklace came off and fell into a cave. I swam down to get it when a huge monster appeared. 'Argh!' I screamed. 'What was that?'
'Don't worry,' the monster said and gave me my necklace.
'Do you want to be friends?'
'OK,' said the monster laughing.
From that day me and the monster were best friends. 'Yay! Monster's here for a sleepover. I'm soo excited!'

Florence Horan (9)
Frieth CEC School, Henley-On-Thames

Meadow Bench

It all started when I was sitting silently on a crooked meadow bench, as the sweet salty smell of sausages soaked through my pages. A young girl approached me, shyly glaring at my favourite diary. As I started to read it, she decided to edge forward closer and closer every second. I explained how much I craved the food from the picnic rasher to rasher. She then walked away, leaving me to melt in my own misery, but she came back with a smile on her face holding hands full of lush food and from then on we became best friends.

Arabella Burns (10)
Frieth CEC School, Henley-On-Thames

WWE History

One day SpongeBob and Patrick decided to tell their friends to go to WWE. They said it made you get a six pack and made you strong. When SpongeBob and Patrick and their friends got there they were shaking in fear. One of the wrestlers named John Cena introduced himself and showed them around. First SpongeBob and his friends went to the training room. Good news, there is a handicap match. Bad news, it is only SpongeBob against two guys. When SpongeBob fought, all his friends cheered him on and he won. A little bit of cheering doesn't hurt much.

Mikey Maciej Howard (9)
Frieth CEC School, Henley-On-Thames

Charlie's Space Adventure

Charlie always wanted to be an astronaut as a child. As Charlie was now an adult he had to get a job so he could be an astronaut. One day Charlie phoned Jim to see if he could get a job as an astronaut. Jim said yes and could he work tomorrow morning. Charlie arrived at the space station. Jim said that Charlie would go on his first space flight in three hours. Later, Charlie was floating around in space. Charlie had just found a new planet that no one had discovered. Charlie named the new planet Luna Guna.

Harrison Griffin Taggart (9)
Frieth CEC School, Henley-On-Thames

Rush To Grandma's House

'Quick, quick, quick,' Unicorndog mumbled to himself. Unicorndog did not want to be late for the Christmas dinner at Grandma's house. He rushed out the door with his umbrella just in case it rained. Unicorndog lived in a place called Pinkville where everything is pink. He got in his car and drove away. Unicorndog was very close to Grandma's house when his car broke down. He was so mad and sad that he would not be able to make it in time. Unicorndog had to walk in the rain to Grandma's house. 'You made it!' shouted Grandma.
They all cheered.

Noah Thomas Munger-Styles (10)
Frieth CEC School, Henley-On-Thames

Roy In Trouble

One cold dark night Roy was walking to the chip shop when there was someone robbing the shop. He sprung into action and tried to stop the thief. He raced along and got the thief out of the building. Suddenly, when he was paying for the chips the police came. For a moment Roy thought he was the thief so he ran. He headed to the highest building in London. Once he came to the top the only way was to jump. The police were closing in. He jumped and landed but the police fell off. 'Done!' said Roy.

Louis Davies (10)
Frieth CEC School, Henley-On-Thames

Help Police!

One summer's day Lilly decided to go to the beach. As she was walking she heard a little girl calling, 'Help!' She rushed over to go and see what was wrong. To her surprise, there was a little girl tied to a tree. Lilly ran towards her. She untied the string that was tightly wrapped around her cold, thin body and asked her name. She was called Sam. She started to cry. Lilly picked Sam up in her arms and wrapped her towel around her, gave her some hot cocoa and walked her back home to her family.

Bertie Trevelyan
Frieth CEC School, Henley-On-Thames

The Magic Spider

'Mum, my friends are coming round tonight so don't mess it up!' said Piper.
'All right,' said Lilly. 'As for you Anne, into my room, I need to talk to you.'
'Hey, what's in that box?' said both the children rather surprised.
They opened it... Then a spider appeared and gave them both three wishes each, like a magic genie. Anne wished to go to Sweety Land. Then they fainted. They were in Sweety Land. Stuck! The genie had erased their memories but their bond with their family was too strong. They remembered and wished themselves home. Cheeky Genie!

Molly Saunders (9)
Frieth CEC School, Henley-On-Thames

The Dream War

James sprinted through the towering trees to meet Joe. However, behind him a dark figure stood and stared... It followed them. They began to run and the shadow fell and grazed himself; he couldn't continue.
There were two left and a bigger chance of them escaping. They could see an exit but it was guarded by another dooming figure. Joe suggested that if they distracted it they could escape. Joe jogged across the dull hallway to distract it; he did.
James opened the hatch and Joe caught up. *Nininini!* His alarm awoke him and his jolly mum, Daisy, came in.

Rosie Humphries (11)
Hill View School, Banbury

The Fairy Who Learnt Her Lessons By Not Being Naughty

Stella is a beautiful fairy but she is very naughty. Stella ran away from the emerald, bejewelled school!
It was so tragic, everyone was trying to find Stella, but she was busy finding a handsome prince. He was called Prince Sam, Stella loved him but he did not love her.
Then, a gorgeous princess appeared and giggled, "Why are you crying?"
Stella replied sadly, 'Because Sam doesn't love me.'
'Well, come to the palace,' my dear. 'My mum's the queen you see.'
Princess' mum helped Stella in getting married to the handsome prince, and they lived happily ever after.

Evelyn Abraham Sunkary (8)
Langdon Academy, London

Prince And A Princess

Once upon a time there was a prince named Jack. He needs to marry a princess so he can be a king and have a beautiful queen. So he went off to rescue a princess from a tower. Through the forest, through the thorns and to the tower, but there was a problem. A dragon was there so Jack fought the dragon. The dragon blasted fire at Jack but Jack used his shield to protect himself and the fire bounced back to the dragon. The dragon was dead and Jack rescued May. They married together happily.

Nathaniel Rodrick Sasikumar (7)
Langdon Academy, London

The Monster House

Once upon a magical time there were two boys called Bob and Zoltar. They were playing basketball where Zoltar's house was. Their ball went to a man's house and the two boys saw the man die.

The next day their uncle went to get his ball and he went inside the man's house. A ghost took him! Finally the man's ghost went inside a bottle so the next day the boys went to the park and they had fun in there. They had a really good time and they lived happily ever after.

Sinthushan Sakthiyalingan (8)
Langdon Academy, London

Harry And The Furious Queen

Pow! Harry kicked the ball at the queen. She got so furious that she shouted, 'Get him!'

So her lazy servants chased after him but he got away and the queen screamed, 'You are so lazy!' She got a spear and threw it at Harry. He ducked and it went over, yet he still didn't stop running. The angry queen threw the sharp spear at Harry and it poked through his shiny football boot. He couldn't move.

The queen asked, 'Why did you do that?'

Harry answered, 'I'm really sorry.'

So the queen let him off and he was safe.

Masroor Rahman (8)
Langdon Academy, London

Timber Vs Pirates

Today is the football match and I'm playing in the match. I am with the pirates, I am the striker. The match is about to start; it is on. As we all know, I am really fast, I also know that Sals, the goalkeeper, can save every single goal.

Now it is half-time. After a bit of a break, Timber starts off but Captain Noeye tackles him and passes to me. I shoot and I score. The game is now finally finished. We have just won the World Cup trophy!

Salsabil Moral (8)
Langdon Academy, London

Eve And Zain

Once there lived a girl called Eve. She had friends called Jana, Electra and Rhydian. They were all in a gang and in college. One day Eve was walking in the hall and a boy took her phone. A boy called Zain ran and got her phone and gave it back. Eve said, 'Thanks.'

'No problem,' said Zain.

Next day Jana and Rhydian said, 'Look Zain!'

Eve waved. Zain went to Eve's table and said, 'Can I text you?'

'Yes,' said Eve.

'Call me,' said Zain.

'OK,' said Eve.

Zain said, 'Marry me?'

Eve said, 'Obviously yes, man!'

Naymah Ali (9)
Langdon Academy, London

Grim And The Cloning Machine

It was my birthday and I got a dog. I called him Grim. I went to my friend Trayurus' later on. Lightning was dancing across the sky. Trayurus built a cloning machine and tried to clone Grim. He tried but it killed Grim. He was just a pile of bones. He then built another machine and I put the bones on the machine and Grim came back to life. I then went home and told Mum about the epic things that had happened at Trayurus' house. I went back there another day and had lots of fun with teleporting machines.

Kaiden Joseph Salmon-Monelle (7)
Langdon Academy, London

Untitled

There was a team called The Toon Titans and one day a bad guy came and took them back in time. They went into Regular Show World and they met a monkey and they said, 'Will you help us make a time machine?'
'Yeah! I will. Where are the instructions? I don't know how to build this. I am going to call Skips from Regular Show to help us. Here she comes!'
'Why don't you look around?'
'Okay, Skips is here already?'
'Finished!'
'Oh bye!'
Bang! Crash! Boom! Now we were back home so let's just go back to sleep!

Makai Graham-Phillips
Langdon Academy, London

All At Sea

Charlie's mum was going shopping. When Charlie's mum went Charlie was bored. His brother John and his sister Lora were sleeping. Charlie decided to go to his football club. After that John and Lora woke up and had breakfast. When Charlie got home they went to the sea. They had lots of fun. When they were going home they saw Mum and because of that they ran home. When Mum came home she had pizza. They ate the pizza and everyone went to the sea again. They had even more fun. After that they went to bed.

Khuzaifa Ali (8)
Langdon Academy, London

Dan And The Cookie Of Truth

A person called Dan visited a village in a peaceful town. He visited the king of the big town. His name was King Arthur with his shiny crown. He asked, 'Dan, can you be a knight for us!'
Dan said, 'Yes, I will be a knight.' When Dan went to get the cookie of truth back from the evil king, before he got there, he had to get through the thunder which danced and the dark forest. When he got there...
'Stop right there!' a soldier said.
Finally Dan beat the evil king easily.

Andrejs Savcuks (8)
Langdon Academy, London

Space Adventure

One sunny day there were two best friends, Tom and Jessica. They loved exploring so they looked into a telescope to see if there were any planets that were nice. They saw a big new planet. They went to the launcher and they got to space and off they went. They found a new adventurous planet. There was lava, water and holes. They flew over the lava, swam through the water and jumped over the holes. At the end of the planet there was a puppy. They took him home and lived happily ever after. 'Goodbye!' they said happily.

Martyna Anna Stryczek (8)
Langdon Academy, London

A New Planet

5, 4, 3, 2, 1... Blast-off! My rocket shook violently. Next thing I knew me and my co-pilot were vanishing into thin air along with my rocket. We re-materialised on a new planet that just formed after a star exploded into a supernova. Lightning danced across the lilac sky. The planet, that multi-bot named Bobbi Sing-Song was deserted. We reached a section where it was covered in snow. The snow was a white blanket. *Bleep!* 'New star discovered.'
'Oh great, that's just what I need,' I grumbled. Then I realised that when we landed my rocket was broken...

Faaiz Saqib
Langdon Academy, London

Mark The Astronaut

'I wish that I could travel to space,' said Mark. Mark had a bubbly personality. He wore a white astronaut top and the same for his legs. Mark built a rocket with a pointy top. He launched up to space quickly. When he saw his favourite planet Mars, without any fear, he went as fast as he could. As fire went all over him, he felt very hot. Even when he put 500ml of water on him, it didn't go away. Unfortunately Mark died. Even though he died, on Earth he was never forgotten by anyone.

Sathujan Amos Sivarajan
Langdon Academy, London

The Treasure Of The Pearl Necklace

There once was a girl called Taria who lived with her parents. Taria said, 'We're going to the beach.' When they arrived Taria went to have a swim. She dived into the deep blue ocean. Taria found a beautiful pearl necklace that was like soft balls attached to each other. Taria put it on and turned into a mermaid, with beautiful long hair, 'It must be the necklace!' she said. Taria dived back into the sea and met new mermaid friends called Maimuna and Fatma. Taria learnt how to be a good mermaid. She lived happily with her friends.

Jamila Surname?
Langdon Academy, London

Invasion From Aliens

On a planet called Saturn were aliens who were invading Earth but ten strong people were determined to stop them. The ten strong people went to Saturn and did what they could do to the aliens. But whatever they did, they still could not destroy the aliens. Only one man could and the one man took one of the alien's solar power guns. One, two, three, four shots and all the aliens were gone. The people on Earth were safe for ever and the ten strong people were famous and were so, so rich.

Yassen Aymadov Ibrahimov (8)
Langdon Academy, London

The Amazing Time Travel

During summer, in Argentina, there lived a boy called Abishoke. He loved building machines. One day he built a time machine. He then travelled to the age of dinosaurs. He was so fascinated. He saw ten small space rocks lying on the floor. Then he had a problem. There was a herd of ankylosaurus running, thinking he was a velociraptor. Then there was an amargasaurus.
After two minutes the ground was boiling hot. While he jumped into the time machine and went away a supernova exploded. That's how dinosaurs died. Then he took the space rocks to school.

Anish Raja
Langdon Academy, London

Robot Joins A Football Team

There lived two football players who were the best ever! They always worked as a team so they always won the World Cup. Everything was fine for that team. The two best players were called Teddi and Sleepy. Soon a robot, who cheats a lot, joined the football team. The robot needed training for one day and that was it. He became the best player of football after his training. But because he was really confused in the real match Teddi won. The robot gave up football because he was really angry. He was searching for another football match.

Florina Muresan (8)
Langdon Academy, London

The Haunted Football Stadium

The football match was about to start between the Cool Tigers and Kings. They were all scared. There were always two monsters on the top of the stadium, a haunted stadium. The match was about to start. Tigers were going for goal. Out of the sky a big monster came. Everyone was so incredibly scared. Later they called the army. They were not available so then they called another army. They came with six tanks. It did not affect the monsters but at the very last minute the jets came throwing bombs at them. They were exterminated.

Aatir Mohamed (8)
Langdon Academy, London

Jake Agesta And Harry Doom

Once upon a time there was a football player called Jake Agesta. He had golden studs and Harry Doom had pink boots. Jake was in Barcelona and Harry Doom was in Bristol City. One day Harry stole Jake's golden studs, and threw the pink boots in the bin. When Jake woke up he was afraid that a ghost took his golden studs. When the match started Jake went on the pitch with bare feet. Suddenly Jake saw Harry with his golden studs so Jake kicked the ball at Harry's feet and Jake caught the shoes and laughed at Harry Doom.

Arian Jashari (7)
Langdon Academy, London

Mysteries Of Egypt

There once lived a prince, his name was Tutankhamun. He wanted to go and explore Ancient Egypt. He got all his stuff, packed a camel, ready to head north. He saw a funny-looking building that was shaped like a triangle but thought he would leave it alone and let people do what they wanted. But as he was walking away, he saw a pretty girl. He asked her name and she replied, 'Jasmine.' He asked her to marry him. After some time they were married and lived in a palace! They had two children and called them Hannah and Arron.

Matthew Gillini (8)
Langdon Academy, London

Superheroes Zofia And Florina To The Rescue

One day there was a superhero called Florina and one called Zofia. They were sisters. Suddenly Zofia and Florina sprang into action. Their mission was to do with something being bulletproof. They defeated the bad guy with a *pow! Boom!* They celebrated at home and they were happy to celebrate their first mission. Suddenly... there was a big boom and their guests were scared. They thought that the super sisters wouldn't defeat the bad guy called Arian. The super girls tried then they remembered the bomb so they put it in front of Arian... They shouted, 'Victory!'

Tiahanna Ogutuga (8)
Langdon Academy, London

World Wars

Once upon a time in New York 120 years in the future with robots and other new technology, things were peaceful until Hitler attacked the prime minister in Turkey. They announced war with New York. There were two little boys called John and Lewis. They were scared of the war, so were their parents. Their house blew up and their mum and dad died. When the bomb dropped Lewis' dad managed to push them into a hole before he died. The bad soldiers were so sad that they gave up. Then New York won and Turkey lost. New York!

Kalan Goyal
Langdon Academy, London

World War 2

Once upon a magical time in England there was an empire who had a leader named Winston Churchill. The enemy was Germany and their revolting leader was Adolf Hitler.
One day England heard a report about a shooting in Berlin so England had to react quickly and Germany came to England. They had to turn around before they could terrorise England and when they got there they struck. Hitler was furious while this was happening. Blackouts and everything was happening.
A year later all of the Germans were toppled and Hitler felt no choice but to shoot himself in the head.

O'Shea Roberts (8)
Langdon Academy, London

Selina's Fruit Pie

Selina was picking all kinds of fruit when suddenly Monkey Max stole a shiny green apple. 'Stop! Come back!' Selina cried. The monkey didn't stop. Selina swung through the jungle but the monkey swung too. 'Oh no I will never make the fruit pie,' Selina sighed. Then something happened. The monkey fell, so Selina grabbed a vine, ran up to the monkey and tied him up. She took the apple.
That night Selina made a fruit pie for all the animals with the fruit that she had gathered. The monkey never stole again. He ended up as a police monkey!

Zofia Cieraszewska (8)
Langdon Academy, London

The Princess And Her Friend

One day a princess went to the woods and met a fairy godmother.
The fairy godmother said, 'Hello, what do you want?'
The princess said, 'I want some new shoes.'
The fairy godmother said, 'You can have anything you want.'
The princess thought, 'I need lots of help,' she said. 'I wish my
stepsisters wouldn't be rude to me anymore.' The princess' wishes
came true.
When the princess returned to her palace her stepsisters were kind
to her. The princess and her stepsisters lived happily ever after.

Mahira Sultana (7)
Newington Green Primary School, London

The Magical Library

Once upon a time there was a girl called Scarlett. She always
wanted to be a librarian when she grew up. As years went by
Scarlett grew bigger, bigger and bigger! She became a brilliant
librarian. One night Scarlett went to her library and she heard
strange noises surrounding her. Windows opened and books fell
off shelves, leaves blew everywhere and Scarlett was petrified!
Suddenly as the wind stopped she saw a ghost. The ghost guided
her into a hole underground. They all had a fantastic ghost party
and got to see each other every night!

Ava Celia Bol (7)
Newington Green Primary School, London

The Three Little Trolls

Not long ago, in the dump there were three trolls and they were called Gruff. One day Little Troll wandered off and saw a bridge. He thought he could have it but there was a huge goat on it. He tried to go across but then... the goat woke up. The troll ran across the bridge but he was too slow and the goat got him. Then he said, 'Please don't eat me!'
'OK then, I won't eat you,' said the goat.
'Thank you.'
But the goat was lying. He ate the troll up!

Kayleb Harry Mustafa (7)
Newington Green Primary School, London

Mermaid Tragedy

Once upon a time, deep under the beautiful sea, there lived a mermaid kingdom! There lived a queen called Charlotte, she had blonde hair and blue eyes.
One day the queen went for a stroll and bumped into a child! The child had red hair and green eyes. The child's name was Roxy. She was a homeless child so the queen took her in. She was very polite and loving! They were very happy together. They loved each other. When Roxy was asleep, Charlotte went into her mum and saw her birthmark! Roxy was the queen's daughter! What will happen next?

Cerys White (10)
New Marston Primary School, Oxford

Mermaid Madness

Once upon a time in the Atlantic underwater kingdom there lived a mermaid, Crystal. Crystal's friends are called Esha, Cerys, Emily and Lea. One day Lea found Crystal hurt on a rock crying. 'Crystal, what happened?' asked Lea.
'The pirates!'
One week earlier, Crystal, the most beautiful mermaid in all the seas went to find her missing dolphin, Aqua. Suddenly a ship appeared. Crystal didn't know what to do. That moment Crystal got captured... The pirates locked Crystal in a room with sharks. Then the pirates dropped her into the sea in a cage. That's how Crystal got hurt.

Ellie Farrell
New Marston Primary School, Oxford

The Dragon's Adventure

A little girl called Lucy went for a walk one day. She arrived at a big cave. She went inside looking amazed. She heard a familiar growl, it was dark. She saw a creature...
It was a dragon, the dragon she met when she was little. She hugged him tight. 'Where have you been?'
He didn't reply.
However, somehow Lucy understood. He went through the woods, fell into a mud pile and killed a lion just to meet her!
'You nearly died for me?'
Finally, after staring into the distance, he said, 'I know...'

Aalia Ahmed (10)
New Marston Primary School, Oxford

The Slave Of The Night

Hi, my name is Hunter and my life hasn't been the same since last month. My eyes are blue and my hair is brown. One day I found a mysterious stone. I picked it up and teleported to Hell from my home in Oxford. I found a girl who whispered, 'My life is depressing. Please help me!'
We found a spell book and used spells to fight monsters and escape. A vampire was stunned and a werewolf was frozen. Eventually we got away and the girl found her parents who were delighted. However, one monster was still alive and extremely angry...

Calum Murray
New Marston Primary School, Oxford

The Magic Ring

On a beautiful day a gorgeous baby girl was born. Her name was Grace. Her mother gave her a beautiful ruby ring but what Grace didn't know was her mother was dying.
Grace grew up wondering where her mother was. Grace ran away being so frustrated. She ran to the forest where she met a boy called Josh. In the forest Grace saw a yellow beehive but Josh was allergic to bees,. Grace was having fun but then she lost her ring. Josh tried to find the ring but got stung by bees and he was never seen again.

Charlotte Armstrong (10)
New Marston Primary School, Oxford

Time Travelling

One day Marcus was sleeping. He woke up and he saw a portal...
In the blink of an eye, he was in a forest hearing big shakes like
earthquakes! Marcus' hair wriggled like worms. Marcus saw a
dinosaur. Running fast, like wind, he saw a house. In the house
was a child his age. He said, 'Do you want food?'
Marcus replied, 'Yes.'
He gave Marcus soup.
'How long have you been here?'
'We have to get to the portal before it closes,' he said. 'Come, let's
go.'
In a flash of lightning a T-rex snatched him quickly.

Omar Iqbal (10)
New Marston Primary School, Oxford

Why, Let's Have A Party!

Ten years ago there was a war with Homer, Marg, SpongeBob,
Stew and Brian. They used pencils to fight and they poked each
other in the eye! They ran to their mums and cried. They had a bet
with a dice man (literally, he was a dice). He was a killer because
he hit people in the head. They said they should give him money,
£21,000,000. They all started jobs, they got £1,000,000 a day!
They all got money. SpongeBob got money and gave it away. He
pooed his pants then he fell over. 'Let's have a party!'

Esha Marong (9)
New Marston Primary School, Oxford

Meeting Friends

Hi, my name is Emma. I moved house. I also moved to a new school. My new school is called St Brooks School. Well , let me get to the point. The first day, I went to my new school I went to the library. I like to read books. I took out a book. I also opened it, and horses, unicorns and lots more animals jumped out! 'What are you doing in here?' a girl asked.
'Nothing!' I answered. I quickly rushed to class. I was scared and shocked about what happened. I was very shocked.

Elyne Freitag (10)
New Marston Primary School, Oxford

Mermaid Tragedy

Once upon a time there lived BFFs Ellie and Maia. They were magical mermaids.One day they met a shark, Esha. Unfortunately Esha poisoned Ellie! Maia was determined to save Ellie before she died. Maia started her quest. The first thing she found was a leaf then a coral, then a rainbowfish. She mixed it up but it didn't work! She was missing a pearl. She used the pearl on her necklace. Maia killed the shark Esha, so she couldn't do it again. Maia started the potion. Warmed it in the oven for ten minutes. She poured it – did it work?

Daniella Knight (9)
New Marston Primary School, Oxford

My Friend's Gone!

Rachel is my best friend but now I need to find a new one.
Rachel was murdered in the dark forest! Nobody knows who did it.
This is how it started.
By the way, my name is Ramal... We were both coming back from
school, you see we're next-door neighbours and our houses are in
the dark forest. Every day we're scared because we hear creaking
noises. However, today they were very loud. We could hear
footsteps, louder and louder until I heard a scream. My feet red
with blood! I looked behind me. Rachel is dead.
Am I next?

Ramal Anas (10)
New Marston Primary School, Oxford

The Man Who Lost His Friends

One day there was a man whose name was Charlie and he was
the lost friend. But one day I saw him as a ghost.
After one month his mum called him and he went all the way to
his mum who lived in Africa. After a while he said, 'All you have to
do is believe in yourself.' I did what he told me to do but it didn't
work. A while ago I tried again and it worked but when I went home
everyone was gone from my life and she had also died.

Esah Akram (10)
New Marston Primary School, Oxford

The Aggressive Alien Army

It's been a few weeks since aliens aggressively turned on us. I'm currently on leave and happily ditched barracks. Life has been hard since Professor Munscul deactivated the 9I5 Atmosphere Security, when the world was at the brink of a disaster. We tried our best to hold the aliens back but they kept coming. Then Earth brought out the big guns! Within a few days it seemed like the army gradually pushed them back. I was as happy as ever! Silence fell, gloomy skies emerged, lives had been eliminated. The bloodshed had ended with great results for Planet Earth.

Ibrahim Alasadi (10)
New Marston Primary School, Oxford

The New Planet

It has been a year since Sam and his gang have been finding a mysterious planet to discover.
Then a few minutes later a mysterious planet popped up on the screen. Sam was surprised and he touched that planet. The planet's name was Pear. When they saw the planet, Sam got ready to go to the planet. As he reached space he saw the planet. When he took his first step into the planet he discovered that it was just like Earth but older. A moment later Sam's rocket was destroyed and zombies and aliens came out... *Boom!*

Joel Jacob (10)
New Marston Primary School, Oxford

Mutants Vs Humans

Deep under the mysterious bone-shivering depths of the ocean there is a swarm of creatures that are scheming a plan to take over the whole universe. They are also creating a liquid that will turn every human being on this planet into creatures like themselves. But there is a gathering of the humans to see what they should do about this invasion of mutant freaks. They decide to fight against the creatures. On the other hand the swarm is getting bigger by the second and the human army is getting smaller by the second. The battle will commence...

Mason Robins (10)
New Marston Primary School, Oxford

Patrick And The Ninjas

Once there was a boy called Patrick. Patrick was obsessed with ninjas, he wanted to be one so much. He had one problem, he was too mean to everyone. But he did have one good side, he knew a ninja. Patrick rang his ninja friend up, 'I want to be a ninja,' Patrick moaned.
'Are you trained?'
'No, but I am prepared,' he said.
'Fine but only if you are good for ever, then you can be a ninja.'
So Patrick cleaned the dishes, walked the dog and cleaned his room every day. Patrick is now an elite ninja.

Archie Duffy-Murphy (10)
New Marston Primary School, Oxford

Invasion

I was only ten when it happened. We didn't expect it, they just came, took over and showed no mercy. However much we tried to stop them, we couldn't. They took the kids and controlled them or killed them. Everyone else went into hiding. In the weeks that followed, they found us and took half. I was lucky to still be alive and not be used to kill the rest of humanity.

Archie Hedger (10)
New Marston Primary School, Oxford

My Weekly Swim

My favourite hobby is swimming. I normally go every Saturday to Marston Ferry. I bob up and down, going to and fro to the deep end. I go to swimming lessons weekly on Tuesdays. We do backstroke, front crawl and loads of other movements. I like treading in water. I like circling my legs. The longest I can do it is for ten seconds maximum. The stroke I dislike the most is backstroke because when I rotate my arms the water gets in my nose. I find my teacher very fair. Steven is his name. I am in Stage 5.

Molly Wambui Ndungu (10)
New Marston Primary School, Oxford

The Superiors

The end is near. Experimentx has taken over Earth. We, the Superiors are Earth's last hope. I, Raptor, Metalfist and Litch will defeat Experimentx. Now we're closing in on his mothership, the Exodus. What we're going to do is destroy the mainframe of the ship, then break in. Litch is firing our detonating missiles at the colossal ship. We've destroyed the mainframe. All we have to do is break in, the toughest part. Finally we made it through. In the darkness we saw his shadow. We heard a sinister, diabolical laugh as he vanished into slender air. Silence.

Alexander Elie Degtiarev (9)
St Joseph's Catholic Primary School, London

Hammersmith And Blitz Line

I stepped onto the train and watched the darkness pass through the windows. I hopped off it onto the station, which looked odd. Why were there old-fashioned people lying on mats? Outside was different too, everything was dark and small, metal huts lined gardens. Suddenly a hand whisked me inside one and I heard a bang! 'You could have been killed by a Jerry! Why are you outside during an air raid?' a woman yelled. I realised I was in 1941, the Blitz! I ran but another hand pulled me and I saw a German, a spy sneering at me...

Genvieve Breen (10)
St Joseph's Catholic Primary School, London

The Terrible Octopus

Once upon a time there was a peaceful underwater world where everybody was living in accord and harmony, until the day a devilish, horrible octopus arrived, spreading terror and fear around. Everyone was petrified by his nasty and furious temper, as he was able to kill just with a hit of its tentacles. Nobody dared to go out anymore.

But one day a brave fish decided to defeat the monster. While the octopus was sleeping, the little fish poked a stick in his eye, blinding him forever. Since then, the octopus never attacked again and they lived happily ever after.

Philippe Seidenberg (10)
St Joseph's Catholic Primary School, London

Past

Beep! Beep! Beep! Waking up from my sleep I couldn't believe my eyes, there was a metal box. What could it be? I looked around the box, there was nothing strange, until I pressed the button and two doors opened. I stepped inside and suddenly two doors closed! Everything was dark, until doors opened. I was confused. Everything was different, old-fashioned people and everything! I peeked through a window and then I noticed that I was in 1935! I looked around, everything seemed exciting so I stayed there and lived there because the time traveller had vanished forever!

Laura Matilde Crocioni (10)
St Joseph's Catholic Primary School, London

Jason's Adventure

A long time ago in a land called Fruitville lived Jason who was celebrating his 9th birthday. But one gift was weird, it had a button saying, *Prehistoric.* He pressed it. *Zap!* 'Ow!' screamed Jason. There was a sound like a crying baby. He looked to his left and saw a huge dinosaur called Corny Dave. In the distance he saw another banana. He was familiar. For the first time Jason rode a dinosaur. They went over to the banana, it was... Grampy Banana! He had been lost and found! Grampy Banana was badly smashed. 'Riley!' he moaned, 'Riley!'

Kieran Brian Connolly (10)
St Joseph's Catholic Primary School, London

Hang On Goard

'Dan, quickly, go fetch me some iron,' ordered Bob, not taking his eyes off his work. I was fed up with dad, he was too tough and I was angry with him! I packed my bags and left.
I went into the forest; outside it was bright and sunny but now it was all as dark as night and it was so misty that you could almost feel it. I didn't like this.
Suddenly, something beneath the trees moved, bushes rustled, two bright yellow eyes stood out from the mist. I stepped back, it had already pounced. Everything was blurred...

Edoardo Speranza
St Joseph's Catholic Primary School, London

Big Hiro 6 2

It was a gloomy day on Orbiter 16 around Uranus. Hiro left the command module to check it out with Big Hero 6, Hiro turned a corner and found Baymax 3.0! Suddenly Krei's son Mat tried to destroy Baymax! Wasabi cuts a hole through the door and all of a sudden they're in loose space! Mat shot a powerful laser at Hiro! Baymax had no choice but to retrieve him. Max went after them both and found that they were on their way back! Max was punched by Baymax's rocket fist and fell to his burning death...

Julian Lumpe Garcia (10)
St Joseph's Catholic Primary School, London

Dicky's Life

It's midday and inside a small hole, small reptiles hatch out of their eggs, leave the hole and run straight to the trees. A group of hungry male dimetrodons chase them. Quickly Dicky and Mooree get to the tree first. Dicky realises how hard life is going to be.
Next, Dicky realises he is hungry and that he has to find food. So he leaves the mound and sets off. On his way he meets an odonata and eats it. Dicky will become a strong and proud predator.

Antonio Gonzalez Napoles (10)
St Joseph's Catholic Primary School, London

Planet Unknown

Lying in bed I heard a noise outside. I looked out of the window, blue fog fell into my eyes. I rushed to my garden and found a UFO with a black figure that ran straight into the bushes. I was very curious to know where it came from. I decided to check clues! I was really tired so I leaned against the side and in no time I was in space. Landing, I went outside and saw an army of aliens. Out of nowhere someone came out of another rocket, killing them all. I thanked him and went.

Jad Awada (10)
St Joseph's Catholic Primary School, London

Tom And His Annoying Brother

Once upon a time there was a boy called Tom and he had a brother called Bill. He was very annoying. Once Bill ripped Tom's very important GCSE papers. Tom and Bill had a cupboard which is magical, you can go to different places. They went to Japan a few days ago and it didn't go that well because Bill pressed a button which would make it disappear. Ninjas started to come near them. Suddenly Tom saw a button in his bag so that they could go home. Bill pressed it and *whoosh,* they were back home. Mission complete!

Sam Norris (10)
St Joseph's Catholic Primary School, London

Untitled

3... 2... 1... I have lift-off. I am in space. While I was enjoying the moment, *bang!* I got sucked out of the ship away from Earth.
The black hole was damaging the ship badly, just like me, it was sucking us in. I was blown into a different dimension where we had to rebuild the ship because it was broken into pieces. If we didn't fix it we would be stranded. I got sent out to fix the crack and I did. We used max power and shot away from the black hole and returned home.

Louis Mareschal-Leduc (11)
St Joseph's Catholic Primary School, London

Untitled

Once there was an ice queen who lived in an ice palace. She only wanted to live in winter. One night, Prince George got lost on his voyage and found the ice palace. He knocked on the door and the ice queen opened it. It was love at first sight. Prince George persuaded the ice queen to live in the Rose Palace which is located in spring.

Abigail Judge (10)
St Joseph's Catholic Primary School, London

Unknown Planet War

It was a sunny day, until the dark inky clouds robbed the light and a spacecraft entered the sky. It was about triple the size of a normal skyscraper. The humans were petrified. Just then the human voice realised there was still a winning chance. The reporter had now confirmed to the army that something was suspicious. During the process the spacecraft got closer. The spacecraft was centimetres away. Then it landed on Earth. The army plotted their fire. Soon enough robots came out, and every member of the army was blinking, all thinking, *what will we do...?*

Philippe Seidenberg (10), Carlo Sebastiani (11) & Daniel
St Joseph's Catholic Primary School, London

Running For My Goal!

This is where it starts, I found my passion... I found my future. This is not like any other dream, it is a hard one to get. You have to work hard and you can never take your eyes off that dream. If you haven't guessed what my dream is, my passion and soon my reality, it is to become an *Olympic athlete!*
As I run in the 600m, I say to myself in pain, 'I can do this, this is what my future depends on,' so as I finish second place, I feel so proud of myself.

Jayda Husbands
St Joseph's Catholic Primary School, London

The Rich Pizza

Once there was a pizza who was pepperoni. He spent all his money on fancy gadgets and cool clothes.
A week later he got a bill of £1,000. He didn't have a penny, no matter how many pickles, hams or salami he put on himself, he couldn't get warm. He tried getting the £1,000 by renting out his oven but he didn't have enough money to pay the bill. He moved to a cheaper oven but he did it again with regrets.
A day later, a giant came to the oven and took him out and ate him without regrets.

Riley William John Corcoran (11)
St Joseph's Catholic Primary School, London

Other Way Around

In a calm small village there was a young girl called Little Red Riding Hood. She was a beautiful, blonde-haired girl.
One day, she went to her grandma's house and brought some food with her just in case. She knocked on the door and waited. 'Come in!' her grandma said quietly. So she walked in and fed her with the food she'd brought with her. Then her grandma fell asleep. Little Red Riding Hood let her sleep for a while and then attacked. She ate her in one big gulp and then, the woodchopper came to help out.

Julia Portka
Sundon Park Junior School, Luton

The Magic Picture

There she was, Amy, just staring at a picture. It made her so happy looking at that beautiful thing. It was a picture of the sea on a sunny day and a happy family playing. 'Honey come and eat your tea!' shouted Amy's mum.
'OK, I will be down in a minute Mum!' explained Amy.
Once Amy had finished her tea, she stomped back upstairs into her bedroom and sat at the end of her bed and looked again. She stood right in front of her picture and suddenly... it pulled her in and she screamed extremely loud.

Lauren Thompson (10)
Sundon Park Junior School, Luton

Cookie Crumble

As Chip, the cookie, shattered along the floor, Crunch, the chocolate, was bugging him . 'I'm the best,' Chip declared in anger. 'I don't know who you're talking to,' declared Crunch with steam pouring out of his ears. The argument went on for the day and will probably go through the night. Suddenly footsteps approached. *Thump! Thump!* 'It's Jeff the cookie monster, argh!' screamed Crunch. *Snap! J*eff had eaten Chip! He was gone. A grave was made outside the Palace of Gum. A flag of candyfloss was made to remember him dearly. Crunch was the best. Yay!

Sophie Claire Hubbard (10)
Sundon Park Junior School, Luton

The Fish That Can't Breathe Underwater

One day there was a fish that couldn't breathe. He didn't like swimming in the sea. How can a fish not like swimming?
The next day the fish rang the builders. The builder came and started building a house for the fish. It was massive. So he lived on land. He had a cooker and a cupboard. Charlie the fish started to admire his house. When he walked into his house he loved the house that Bob the Builder built.

Keane Spriddle (10)
Sundon Park Junior School, Luton

The Skeleton Battle

As Commander Cameron shot towards Jupiter a UFO shot missiles at him so he flew as fast as he could. When he landed Emma Golfish (the witch) tried to destroy him. She had freeze breath and Commander Cameron could shoot fireballs from his hands and he could fly. Emma Golfish had a cobweb dress so anything could stick to it and she could turn invisible.The commander's UFO can go 9,000,000 miles per hour and has long missiles and lasers. On Jupiter there were Eskimo zombies and a massive skeleton called Skeletron. He fought the Eskimo zombies and beat them all in a battle to rule Jupiter.

Cameron Jay Dennett (10)
Sundon Park Junior School, Luton

The Attic

There was once four children, Dylan, Lauren, Amy and Zaina. They were all brothers and sisters. They were all happy until Amy noticed the attic. She asked her mum if she could look inside but her mum said no!
One day her auntie came and that was their opportunity. At night they snuck up the stairs, onto the landing and into the attic. Suddenly the door closed behind them. Then a giant candyfloss clown stomped in front of the doorway that went back to home. 'I am Kai!' shouted the clown.
'What have you done Amy?' exclaimed Dylan.'
'Watch out!'

Katherine Davey (9)
Sundon Park Junior School, Luton

Einstein Is Now Dumb!

On a suspicious day, the smartest man in the world, Einstein, woke up on the wrong side of the bed. Now he was warming up for his daily maths test and the first question, 9 + 10, he couldn't work it out. He was puzzled. As he went into the lab to cook something up that could make him smart, he couldn't remember how to make it. So he asked one of the other scientists and they didn't believe him. But after a good night's sleep he was back to his old brilliant, smart self.

Ellis Coffie (10)
Sundon Park Junior School, Luton

The Three Doors

He stumbled into the library. 'Hello is body any there?' he said, getting his words mixed up as always. No answer. Ahead of him he saw a sign. He read it. It said: *Pick A Door Because The Walls Are Closing.* Panicking, the door slammed shut and the walls started to close. With shaking hands, he reached for the third door in sight. He trembled. As the door swung open, he found himself staring at a gargantuan rhino. 'Blaaaaaagh!' he screamed. As the rhino came charging at him, he covered his eyes in fright. Just then it turned into a donkey!

Dylan Reeves (10)
Sundon Park Junior School, Luton

The Magic Fiver

Emma took her last fiver out of her bag as she entered the sweet shop. She walked in and bravely bought a handful of sweets. Now, she had no money left. Or so she thought... On the way home, she walked past the cinema. She badly ached to go in! Checking her bag, she found her magic fiver was back! Amazed, she paid for her entry ticket. After the film, she went bowling with her friend. She had so much fun, she stayed all day. At home, she looked for the fiver. It'd vanished! Something came through the letterbox. Bills...!

Amy Mandayaya (10)
Sundon Park Junior School, Luton

Other Way Around

In Arendelle, Olaf was playing with Sven. He went in the winter forest, he began to melt. But when he got in the warm cosy village he didn't. Then they went to the mountain where it was cold. 'I can't go, I'm going to melt!' Olaf said. Then Elsa put a rainbow on his head so he couldn't melt. So they ran. Marshmallow was there, he was the new king of the mountains. He suddenly began to shrink. Everyone started to laugh at him. Olaf ran after him and made him feel happy and he was crowned king.

Tanisha Khanom (10)
Sundon Park Junior School, Luton

No More Chocolate

Billy found an old teapot at the bottom of a small box in the attic. As he was taking the teapot down the stairs, he dropped it and glass dropped everywhere. Then a blue genie appeared at the bottom of the stairs. Billy had been granted one wish. He wished for a lifetime of chocolate. It came true. 'Why have you gotten so fat?' asked his mum.
'I didn't realise I'd put on the weight.'
After a week of chocolate, he got caught red-handed. Billy's mum had snapped, 'No more chocolate, you're grounded for a whole 24 days!'

Zaina Mirza (9)
Sundon Park Junior School, Luton

No More Peanut Butter

As Sasha woke up she felt like having a peanut butter sandwich. When she came down she had a big argument with her brother and he broke the peanut butter jar. Sasha screamed. Then her mum said there was more peanut butter but it was alive... Sasha ran, this was the only time she ran. She never ran. She couldn't run any further, the peanut butter overtook her. She was doomed. 'I love you brother Max, you are the best brother ever, I love you. I am going to die, help me now...'

Sydnee Farney-Wood (10)
Sundon Park Junior School, Luton

Catastrophe

There was once a colossal Siamese cat that was as fat as a football! His name was Fat Tony. Fat Tony was a very rare Siamese cat due to the fact that he had vertical, straight, orange and black lines. He looked like a tiger. His owner, Amy, made the best puddings ever. Out of the corner of his eye he spotted a mouth-watering chocolate pudding. He accidentally ate the cake. Amy was furious, therefore she put Fat Tony in a detrimental pound full of cruelty. From then on Fat Tony was never, ever, ever to be seen again.

Tasnima Rahman (10)
Sundon Park Junior School, Luton

Tracy's Worry

OK here it goes, type in your worry: I want my mum to see me in the Christmas play. I knew this isn't usually me but I'm a bit scared. All of a sudden, Mr Speed came and peered at it. 'Well Tracy, I'm surprised that you have a worry!'
I explained to Mr Speed that I wanted my mum so much that I would give anything if she could see my play! And guess what? Mr Speed said he would arrange it all for me!
The next week was the Christmas play and my mum came to see me!

Amina Imran (10)
Sundon Park Junior School, Luton

The Galactic Clash

There was once a thirteen-year-old super boy named Adam.
He plays for Galactic FC. They're the best team in the whole galactaverse. They were entered into a draw and were pulled out of the hat to be entered into the Space Raiders Cup. They have made it through the group stages, knockout stages, last sixteen, quarter-finals, semi-finals and now to the finals they go. They had just found out their rivals made it into the finals as well. It would be a hard test for them now. It ended in Galactic FC's favour by winning.

Kieron Leelodharry (10)
Sundon Park Junior School, Luton

Minions Vs The Simpsons

'Help! Help!' bellowed Homer, 'the minions are about to attack Springfield.' Then the Simpsons get ready to attack back.
'Kevin, ready?' asked Gru. 'Bob, ready?'
'Yes Sir.'
Then everyone furiously charged into Springfield and started attacking. All of a sudden the minions came flying through the walls of Springfield. The only weapon Springfield had was Willie's rake that he used for leaves. Unfortunately most of Springfield's people died from the minions. There was only five Simpsons left after the fight. There was Homer, Bart, Maggy, Willie and Mr Burns. They tried to hide but unfortunately they were aggressively killed.

Freddie Alex Seeby (10)
Sundon Park Junior School, Luton

The Mermaid Married To A Human

'Happy birthday!' said Julia.
'I am 21, yes, yes, yes!' I replied.
'This is the year you get married to a merman.'
'A merman?' I replied.
'Yes,' said Julia.
I swam down into the crystal sea, where I saw the boat. I popped up. I had to be quick because I can only stay out of water for ten seconds. I lost count as soon as I saw his face. My skin started to melt like honey. I knew we were meant to be so I made a wish and he was a merman. Then we got married!

Stephanie Ogbuagu (10)
Sundon Park Junior School, Luton

A Magical Adventure

One day two girls called Lilly and Sophie were walking in the park and found a deep hole. They started to look down the hole and Lilly fell in. 'Lilly,' shouted Sophie, 'I will come down!' exclaimed Sophie. Sophie went down the hole to get Lilly. 'I am coming Lilly!' said Sophie. *Boom!* They fell on top of each other.
'Are you OK?' asked Lilly.
'Yes, are you?' replied Sophie.
'Where are we?' said Lilly.
'I don't know,' replied Sophie.
'Hi there!' said a voice.
'Who are you?' asked Sophie
'I'm Smiley,' replied Smiley.
'Let's be friends,' said Sophie.
'Yes.'

Niamh Amy McGrath (10)
Sundon Park Junior School, Luton

Crash Bandicoot

Crash and his sister Coco were making TVs. Then Doctor Doom kidnapped Coco and it's up to Crash Bandicoot to save her. Crash went on an adventure, running and jumping. Crash also had to fight mystical creatures. Then finally he found Coco in a cave in Doctor Doom's office. Crash had to save her. Doctor Doom put traps around the building and Crash dodged all the traps. He made it to the last floor then he defeated Doctor Doom. Then they went home and carried on with an invention to make more TVs. That's spectacular!

As-Sami Hussain (10)
Sundon Park Junior School, Luton

The S S Spiral

The Spiral was a ship. Everyone went on but it was haunted by a child.
One day it was creepy, one of the passengers fainted and described a little something paper-thin and a green fog. The boat started sinking. People panicked, it slowly sank. People froze in the cold water. No lifeboats came back to save the dying people. The people died. The ship fell under the water, it kept sinking. The people died onboard. Sinking, the engine died, it stayed on the ocean floor. The ship started moving on the floor and returned to harbour.

Jakob Harding (10)
Sundon Park Junior School, Luton

Why Superman Wears Underwear On Top

There once was a superhero who saved the world 70,000 times. One day Superman was flying, then he heard a loud scream for help. It was Miss Kippling. She said, 'Help, my cat is stuck up a really big tree!'
'I will save you,' said Superman. So Superman dived down to save the cat. As he arrived he saw the cat, he picked it up. While he was flying with the cat he felt a breeze. Suddenly he was flying naked! The cat had pulled a loose thread, untangling his whole suit, leaving him buck naked!

Monét Miller (10)
Sundon Park Junior School, Luton

Alert! Barbie Invasion!

On another overcrowded day in a village named Springhills, all was quiet, until now! *Kaboom!* 'Argh! Someone just set off a nuclear bomb!' screamed the villagers.

'It was us, the Barbies! We are here to destroy you!' shouted a Barbie in a pink ballerina dress. The villagers burst out laughing. 'Don't laugh at us or we'll invade your land and do this!' bellowed a Barbie in a tutu. The swarm of minute Barbies jumped as high as they could and super-kicked the village leader so hard that his eyeballs came out of their sockets!

'My flies, I mean my eyes!'

Jake Reeves (10)
Sundon Park Junior School, Luton

Proms And Princesses, Not!

I don't like dresses! I have to wear one to the prom but there's no prince! There is one prince, he's OK but he spends all his time with his unicorn Shannon! Big No! I can't stand the fact of people staring and looking at me. So embarrassing but not as bad as frilly dresses! My dad, Kia, who is married to my mum, Kayleyn, loves me to go to fancy parties. I decided to quit being a pretty princess. I want to just have a better life with my seahorse dogs in the land of deep blue Crazywood. Totally!

Nevaeh Burford (10)
Sundon Park Junior School, Luton

The Magic Cloth

Once upon a boring life, a girl called Nevaeh lived in Boringwood. One boring day she found a boring cloth. It had dull abilities, a dull colour and dull material. Basically it was dull.
But one not boring day, Nevaeh was cold and wrapped the damp old cloth around her. Then, she went to sleep. In the strangely exquisite morning, she woke to find herself stranded in the turquoise sea. She went to move her legs but found that they were unexpectedly fused together. She was a mermaid! From that day on she lived happily ever after (or did she?).

Shannon Mapp (10)
Sundon Park Junior School, Luton

The Fantastic Superheroes

Once upon a time there lived a group of superheroes. They lived in the queen's palace because they are special. 'I think we have a mission to do!' exclaimed Cristal.
The next day they set out on their mission. 'Come on! Keep up.'
'Help! Help!'
'Can you hear that?'
'Yes I can, what is it?' said Willow'
'Look a house!'
'I don't think so, let's have a closer look.'
The superheroes went in the mysterious building. 'Hey guys, Lizzy!' They ran holding on and in a flash they got back home. They had a celebration and lived happily forever.

Louise Isaacs (9)
Sundon Park Junior School, Luton

Woodlice Attack!

Once upon a time, in the town of Beemovia, there lived a boy called Ben. He was really scared because the killer woodlice were attacking. They were eating everything that came into their sight! They were as scary as SpongeBob. Only one thing could stop those beasts and that was the hose of dastardly death to blast the woodlice, sending them to live on the stars with only the sky for company. Everyone on the street was so thankful they gave him every last penny of their money.

Jake Andrew Hosey (10)
Sundon Park Junior School, Luton

Time Tragedy

'Let's play hide-and-seek!' requested George and Ellie.
'No that's for little kids,' replied Peter.
'Please!'
'OK fine!1... 2... 3...'
George and Ellie dashed into their bedroom and concealed themselves in a cupboard. They took several steps backwards and found themselves in a time machine.
'This place is amazing!' bellowed George.
'Don't touch a thing,' warned Ellie. But she was too late. Within milliseconds, they found themselves in Paris.
'Liberté! Égalité! Fraternité!' A mob of irate citizens chased the mysterious object. George pressed another button. Suddenly they found themselves in a futuristic world. Unfortunately, their journey never ended.

Michael Wasido Sungu (10)
Sundon Park Junior School, Luton

Candy Chaos

In a land called Candy Crush lived the most cheery bunny ever.
Her name's Annabelle. Candy Crush was a land of sweets. It
had a variety of treats, from jaw-breakers to candy canes. Candy
Crush had it all. Annabelle's family had a gargantuan green house
cramped with bubble trees. Every day they picked them. Annabelle
noticed something mysterious happening.
One day Annabelle went to pick bubblegum. She saw a muscular
giant stuffing its face with bubblegum! 'I knew something was
happening!' Annabelle said triumphantly. She ran away. The giant
ate the whole land of Candy Crush and became *extremely* fat!

Amy Soeng (10)
Sundon Park Junior School, Luton

Animal Escape

The three fairies had a pet each. They went to feed them and they
were gone! The fairies knew that their pets had magic powers. The
fairies thought they might have escaped with their magic powers.
The fairies were planning a party for the king and queen. 'We need
to find them!' cried Penny.
'Shall we go on an adventure?' beamed Lilly.
'Yes that's a great idea!' replied Katie. So they went on their
adventure.
Two hours later they found their pets. They got to the party at 7:30
and everybody had a great time.

Amie Draper
Sundon Park Junior School, Luton

Adventure Of The Baby Twins

Baby Man flew through the sky, he saw a rainbow and said, 'Look Super Baby there's a rainbow!'
'Cool!' said Super Baby, but suddenly the rainbow turned evil! It turned an old man into an evil rainbow goon who attacked Baby Man. Baby Man bellyflopped him and he fell to the ground and died.

Jhemari Gunn-Nembhard (10)
Sundon Park Junior School, Luton

Time Travelling Trouble

Once upon a time there was a boy called Jeff. He was an ordinary schoolboy who likes adventure! After school he went for a walk in the woods and found a time machine. He could go back in time to 1983, 1984 and loads more. When he got home he got shouted at a bit and was grounded for two days.
One day later he sneaked in the time machine. He went back to 1984. He must be in big trouble. He then met a man called Raven, he went to the time machine and got back home. Phew!

Daniel Begley (10)
Sundon Park Junior School, Luton

The Enchanted Forest

One day a girl called Lauren went to the field and saw an enchanted forest. She went inside and found fairies. She was amazed. One of the fairies showed her around and introduced herself and they had so much fun. Her favourite fairy was Fluttershy.
Over the next few months they became best friends. They did everything together.
One day Lauren's parents got offered a job in America and they couldn't say no to that. So they moved and the two friends were separated and never saw each other again. Lauren and Fluttershy were so upset and wished they were together.

Lauren Williams (10)
Sundon Park Junior School, Luton

Space Planet Pluto

There once lived two aliens and they lived on the moon so they decided on an adventure into space. They saw a spaceman but they thought he was a monster so they kidnapped the spaceman and took him to the planet Pluto. The spaceman who was kidnapped ran to his space shuttle and played a game of cheese. He played with a monkey that loved cheese and ate all of the cheese that was on the table.
The next day the monkey ate the table which happened to turn into cheese and went home happily.

Oliver Benjamin Nunn (10)
Sundon Park Junior School, Luton

Space Age

It was 2600 when a brother and sister named Alfie and Amie were travelling through space. Suddenly they crashed into the moon. They were stranded there and their spaceship broke down. Alfie and Amie found two friendly aliens named Oliver and Lewis. The four friendly people made an epic super spaceship. Alfie and Amie thanked Oliver and Lewis for helping and took off to continue on their journey.

Ria Hunter (10)
Sundon Park Junior School, Luton

Minecraft Mermaids

There was once two Minecraft mermaids (BFFs). They were planning on going on another sea adventure but this time they were trying to find the blue whale. They were setting off into the sea, they had to pack their diamond sword. 'Oh my gosh!' Pinky bellowed, 'look it's our old boat!' So they both decided to go by boat, well, after some repairs.
After ninety minutes of travelling, they had arrived but the whale hadn't. They were trying to figure out what went wrong but this was their first adventure. They hadn't finished...

Tiger-Lily Cronin (10)
Sundon Park Junior School, Luton

Magical Mia's Mistakes

There once was a girl called Mia who lived in Landchantia where everyone was nice and kind. Mia felt hungry and went to the beefhouse. After a delicious meal she went to the woods but she wasn't allowed, it was the rules. Suddenly a great big devil fairy struck thunder. Magic Mia was stuck. She was really scared and called through her watch. It didn't work. So she tried herself. Mia ran as fast as she could and used her magic. She thought it wouldn't work but it did. Mia swore to never go in the woods again.

Millie Das (10)
Sundon Park Junior School, Luton

Enchanted Fairy

Once upon a time, there was a fairy, she was called Renay. Nobody liked her. She was the most spiteful person in the forest. One day she went into the forest and saw the most wonderful thing – the magical bear who brings peace and love to the enchanted forest. The bear was disgusted with her attitude, the bear spoke to Renay about her behaviour. She flipped, she got so angry she burnt down the forest. She was devastated!
She said sorry to the bear and the fairies. They made the forest better and they lived happily ever after. Yay Renay!

Rejonte Dolan (10)
Sundon Park Junior School, Luton

Three Children Crossing The Bridge

Once there were three children called Jamie, Bob and Rob. Every day they played in the field. They knew that it was was full of candy on the other side so were going to attempt crossing the bridge today.
Bob went over first. 'My candy?' spoke the candy monster.
Bob exclaimed, 'My brother's got candy.' Bob trotted along.
Jamie came along. 'Candy?' shouted the candy monster.
Jamie exclaimed 'My bother's got more candy.' Jamie skipped along.
Finally Rob came along. 'Where's my candy?' screamed the candy monster.
Rob ended up eating the candy monster and running to find his friends.

Sienna Healy (9)
Sundon Park Junior School, Luton

Tom Gates Embarrassing

I woke up at 8, which is later than normal. So I was rushing. My friend Derek's dog was barking, his name is Rooster. I finally got my clothes on and leave the house for school. In maths everyone is ignoring me. Marcus, Amy and even Mrs Warrington. I ignore them and get on with my work. It was times table squares. I hate times table squares. I did OK, I think. Probably not because I never do good at times table squares. Break time and everyone was laughing at me. I was wearing my sister's Barbie dress. Oh dear!

Jovanie Brown (10)
Sundon Park Junior School, Luton

The Dolphin Princess

Splash! In and out of the ocean like a torpedo! 'Ow! I'm sorry,' cried a figure.
'No worries. I'm Twighla!' After their hellos, Prince Lightnin whisked Twighla away to his castle! She had a fabulous time at his home castle! But Lightnin's father had known she was the dolphin princess! Little did Lightnin know his father was to kill Twighla! He hid his knife in his pocket and set off to kill! But Twighla was in contact with her guard, Andi. She hurried to save her ruler! No more King De... Never mind. They went to live in Splashafronia!

Mia Stringer (10)
Sundon Park Junior School, Luton

The Unexpected Encounter

It was the year 2021, when a modern spaceship had made the journey to another galaxy and was almost halfway back to Earth. Onboard, a security guard named Owen was accompanied by his two nieces, Alex and Tianna. Suddenly everything died, power gone!
Owen and the two children rushed to the evacuation pods. All gone! Then the three loners travelled by jetpack to the Ender Planet, a new world. The Species were giant slender beasts with teleportation devices. Fortunately the aliens, called Endermen, lent a teleportation pearl to each person. They used these to teleport to Earth.

Jack Lewis Kaufman (11)
Sundon Park Junior School, Luton

Untitled

One day it was a stormy day under the water. It was terrible because the creatures in the water were fed up with the weather because it was annoying. When it was morning the creatures in the water were up but the weather stopped, then it was sunny for them. The water was shiny on the top and it shone under the water. Suddenly a hammerhead shark came and ate all the yummy tasty fish. But some fish swam away.

Amelia Eldridge (10)
Sundon Park Junior School, Luton

Untitled

It was the year 2525 when Planet Earth was revolutionised. Everyone lived a happy life in the new world. Unfortunately, one person, Max, was anxious because he was going to space to observe the ISS. However, he was only an amateur spaceman. Space was never visited since 2040 which was a problem. Finally, the day arrived. Max and his colleagues, Weaver and Alexander, were shooting up to space. In the next twenty minutes they were in space in the ISS, Suddenly, it broke down by an alien spaceship. Nevertheless, it was not a threat, they became friends and fixed it.

Caleb Githua (10)
Sundon Park Junior School, Luton

Ballet Exam

I stood outside the ballet studio. It was the same place I had practised many times before but this was different. I knew I was well-rehearsed. I had run through the scenario in my head. I was still scared and worried. I was called in. The lady looked like my grandma and smiled at me. She said I looked like her grandson. She asked me to do my routine. As soon as I started I was in my comfort zone. I was floating on air. It felt good, 83 out of 90. I was ecstatic by the end.

Finn Mayhew Smith (8)
Westfields Junior School, Yateley

The Cup Final

It was the day of the Cup Final. Everyone in Yateley was very excited. Finally the referee blew his whistle to start the game. Ten minutes in and it's still nil-nil. No, wait! Rhys is on the edge of the box, turns, shoots, scores! Half-time has arrived and it remains one-nil.
Second half's underway and straightaway our team scores again. Ten minutes later we score again to make it three-nil. With five minutes remaining we lose a goal, making it a nervous final few minutes. But we hang on to win the Cup... three-one!

Rhys Reardon-Davies (8)
Westfields Junior School, Yateley

Ocean Sea Planet

In the space station there was a spaceship called Zoomer Comet. It was about to set off in
5... 4... 3... 2... 1... *Blast-off!* Speeding through space. When all he could see was an enormous ocean blue planet. So he landed his spaceship on it. Everything was blue! He decided he was going to explore. The ocean was deep but calm. Interesting sea creatures tickled his toes and jumped over his head. What an amazing place to live. He decided to explore more tomorrow. It was time for a good night's sleep. More adventures tomorrow.

Charlotte Moore (8)
Westfields Junior School, Yateley

Cleo's Adventure

Cleo is on a school trip at the museum. She heads off with Alfie in search of the Egyptian section. As she arrives at the Egyptian section, she sees a mysterious mummy. Behind the mummy was an interesting crystal. She presses the crystal, turns invisible and teleports to Egypt. Then she puts down the crystal and the pharaoh takes it and puts them in a prison full of slaves! They starved for four hours so they could fit through the bars, then they could. They fought the pharaoh, got the interesting crystal, pressed the crystal and went back to the school trip.

Isabella Pennington (7)
Westfields Junior School, Yateley

Sonic Adventures

One cloudy day Sonic and Silver were at Silver's hideout, they were checking if Dr Eggman has caused any trouble in the palace city. They found that Eggman had sent his robot minions to capture the chaos emeralds. Sonic and Silver rapidly ran to the teleporter and teleported to the city. When they got there the city was already half destroyed. They went to find Eggman. When they found him he had the emeralds. Silver picked the robots up with his power, threw them at Eggman and destroyed him. Sonic grabs the emeralds and they telported back to Silver's lair...

Nathan Williams (8)
Westfields Junior School, Yateley

The Spooky Doll

Once there was a cottage. Who's inside? Inside was a little girl called Annabelle but she wasn't an ordinary girl. She was a doll, a spooky doll. Mr and Mrs Kaneland loved hanging dolls up on the wall.
One day they took the doll to a shop to sell. The funny bit was she was in a pram! Unfortunately the pram went away on its own. 'Nooo! Get the pram!' Mrs Kaneland said. They ran onto the road to get the pram. Suddenly Mr and Mrs Kaneland got squashed by a car. So now you know the horror story.

Anyulwexeya Makunura (8)
Westfields Junior School, Yateley

Messi's Tale Of A Day

Hi, my name is Messi and I'm a python. I am going to tell you about my day.

First, I woke up after a long sleep. I really did not want to get out of bed but I had to get ready for school. As I was slithering to school, I noticed something bright blue moving in the plants. It was an anaconda. He told me his name was Thiago and today was his first day at school. He was a little bit frightened. 'I'll look after you,' I said. We became best friends and have had lots of adventures.

Jack Randall (8)
Westfields Junior School, Yateley

Nancy's Holiday

Once upon a time there was a little girl on holiday with her family. The little girl was called Nancy. Nancy and her family had gone to the desert and in the desert Nancy found a cactus. She touched the cactus and her finger started to bleed because she touched the spikes. Nancy wanted to give the cactus a name. She named it Spikes. Nancy dug up Spikes and took it home with her in her suitcase. When she planted it in a pot and put it on her window sill it got stolen by her evil sister and she cried.

Yazmin Rae Neville (8)
Westfields Junior School, Yateley

The Story Of Snowy And Snowflake

There was a mischievous fluffy penguin called Snowy. He went to the shops, Snowy saw a girl buying a packet of crisps, it was the last bag... He snatched the packet off the girl Snowflake because he wanted it. His headmaster was just coming into the shop and saw what happened. The girl was disgusted about what happened and walked out of the shop.

The next day the headmaster saw Snowy with the crisps. His headmaster approached Snowy and told him what he saw in the shop. Snowy was given detention. He felt very guilty for what he had done.

Megan Mea Jeffery (8)
Westfields Junior School, Yateley

The Big Worm

One day Peter painted some superheroes but they came to life. There was a big worm. These were the superheroes: The Thing, Spider-Man, Thor and Blade. Together they got the worm. The worm went back underground. The heroes went back home. Spider-Man's head started to tingle, that meant the big worm was back! He rang the other heroes. They came to help. Blade stabbed the big worm in the heart. Thor went back to Asgard.

Oliver Hoare (7)
Westfields Junior School, Yateley

Tallula's Tales

One day my family and I took our puppy Tallula out for a walk in the forest. She was digging holes and suddenly she found a big egg. We took the egg home and put it in a cupboard. Some time later the cupboard shook and went *bang!* There was a dinosaur standing there. The dinosaur and Tallula became best friends. The nasty old lady next door hated them playing and shouted mean things at them. Suddenly the dinosaur had had enough. He jumped over the fence and gobbled the lady up. Tallula and the dinosaur could now carry on playing!

Finley Reilly (8)
Westfields Junior School, Yateley

The Best Lego Friends Ever

Once upon a time there were four sisters named Aerial, Olivia, Emma and Naya. They lived far away in a dark forest. One day, a group of sisters came along named Isabella, Ella and Mia. When Emma first saw them she thought they were mean but they weren't, they were lovely.
Later they had tea together. Ella accidentally spilt two cups when the others weren't looking. 'What was that?' said Olivia.
'It was Mia!' Ella cried.
Olivia knew something was not right and shouted to Ella, 'Get out!'.
Shortly after, Ella returned and apologised to everyone so they forgave her.

Hollie Billhardt (8)
Westfields Junior School, Yateley

Sleepover

It was Friday evening. Zoe came to Amy's house, she felt excited as this was her first sleepover. When she arrived Amy took Zoe to her bedroom to unpack her bag, including sweets for the midnight feast that had to be kept a secret. Suddenly Amy's dad came up the stairs to let them know it was bedtime. They closed their eyes and fell asleep. Amy woke up at 5am, Zoe was already awake. Then they ate sweets together.

Two hours later Mum called them for breakfast but they weren't hungry. It had been the very best sleepover ever!

Amy Gray (8)
Westfields Junior School, Yateley

The Best Sleepover Ever!

There were three girls, Ena, Charlotte and Megan. They are having a sleepover at Charlotte's house. What their mums didn't know was that they had planned to sneak out to the dance. Midnight came and Charlotte tiptoed like a mouse, grabbed the rope and with their pretty dresses they climbed out of the window. At the dance all they did was dance, dance. At 5am they left the dance and went back to Charlotte's house and went to bed. They only had two hours sleep but they felt fine. Do you think they will do it again?

Ena Poskovic (7)
Westfields Junior School, Yateley

The Two Heroes

There was a noisy place where Moshi monsters lived. The noise was so disturbing that Doctor Strangeglove took lots of Moshis to his palace. Two of them escaped – Busling and Georgia. They sat down and thought how they could help. Together they walked to Doctor Strangeglove's palace. Georgia had a special tonic to turn Doctor Strangeglove into a Moshi rabbit. He appeared from nowhere, Georgia chucked the tonic at Doctor Strangeglove. He turned into a Moshi rabbit. All the other Moshi monsters cheered. They all lived happily ever after in Doctor Strangeglove's palace.

Georgia Connor (8)
Westfields Junior School, Yateley

Charlie Saves The Day

Toddington Cup Final, the whistle blows. Tatley Tornadoes vs Blackwell Bullets, rivals on and off the pitch, the tension is high. During half-time Sam the Tornadoes' goalkeeper trips and injures his leg. Charlie, Tommy the striker's best friend, is now put in goal. The Tornadoes were anxious to know what would happen as Charlie was not the best keeper they had. The final whistle blew and it was a draw, now it was down to penalties! Charlie had saved the day, what a result! The Cup was finally coming home with the Tatley Tornadoes. 'Clever Charlie,' they all chanted.

Finley Sage (8)
Westfields Junior School, Yateley

The Final Battle With Herobrine

A brave boy named Steve walked along a dusty path. He found a dark portal made from spinning obsidian. Steve jumped through the portal knowing something bad was happening. Before the portal could be destroyed by his evil arch-nemesis Herobrine, Steve flew out of the portal. Herobrine teleported the portal blocks to his house to trap Steve. A battle commenced using their magic diamond swords. Steve used his special building powers to trap Herobrine into a solid iron cage, where he was imprisoned forever. Steve summoned the obsidian portal with the power of his mind, leading him home.

Hari Moon (7)
Westfields Junior School, Yateley

New York Dogs

In the nice town of Morristown four bored dogs called Jamie, Flash, Peanut and Jack were looking for adventure. They jumped on a train heading to New York City. When they arrived they felt excited and thrilled to be in such an enormous city. They started to explore the busy and chaotic streets looking at the tall buildings, shops and yellow taxis. Peanut was busy sniffing out the hot dog stalls and lost his friends. Jamie, Flash and Jack were worried about their missing friend and looked for him everywhere. They eventually found him sitting in a Lamborghini Reventon. Show-off!

William Lovelock-Moore (8)
Westfields Junior School, Yateley

Daniel The Pharaoh In Egypt

In the desert a pharaoh called Daniel is lost and has been walking around for days trying to find his friend. He is tired and thirsty. Daniel is just about to sit on the hot sand and give up when he saw a tomb. He walked in silently. He saw dead mummies! They looked all dark and cold. He saw shining jewellery in a treasure chest. Daniel could hear a noise coming from another room. He walked through there, his friend Jacob was standing. 'Where have you been?' Daniel crumbled onto the floor crying, relieved he had found his friend.

Kayla McMullen (8)
Westfields Junior School, Yateley

The Whimpering Sound

Toby was cycling through the incredible woods near his house. Suddenly, he heard a noise and stopped his bike. In the distance he could hear a whimpering sound. He started walking carefully towards the sound, the brambles were making it very hard to walk in a straight line. In the corner of his eye he saw a secret passageway, so he quickly ran towards it, there was a dog caught in a cage. The dog didn't seem very happy so Toby released him from the cage. He made his way home with his new friend Buster.

Hayden Charles Lynch (8)
Westfields Junior School, Yateley

Time Travel Hamster

There was a little hamster called Bob with ginger fur, he lived in Yateley pet shop. Bob loves his ball because it magically travels to ancient times. Bob once went into his magic ball which started spinning. He closed his eyes. When he opened them he was inside an Egyptian tomb. Nenet and Neith, the mummification team are there. Suddenly in a flash the door opens and Tutankhamun enters, he demands, 'Wrap Bob up in silk bandages for the afterlife.'
Bob starts shaking so much he can't move. Wrapped like a mummy he sees the pharaoh steal the ball!

Lexi Hogben Stephenson (8)
Westfields Junior School, Yateley

Martha And Jake

Once upon a time in a village lived siblings called Martha and Jake. Their parents were poor so Jake and Martha went to the forest to get some food. There, they got lost and were caught by the wicked witch. They were treated like slaves and were about to be eaten when Martha gathered the courage and pushed the evil witch into burning fire. Jake grabbed her magic wand and they ran back home to their loving parents, who were happy to see their children. The wand helped them get food they needed badly. They all lived happily ever after.

Maja Pejovic-Barnett (8)
Westfields Junior School, Yateley

The Adventure With The Tooth Fairy

There was a little girl who wondered what a tooth fairy would do. One night the tooth fairy came, she waved her wand and said, 'Sparkle and shine, have wings like mine.' The little girl tingled all over and *whoosh* she was the same size as the fairy. They held hands and flew to other houses collecting teeth, reading charming notes and delivering shiny coins. Before she knew it the sun was beginning to rise and it was time to go home, back to her warm, cosy, snuggly bed. Now she knows what a tooth fairy does.

Daisy Tinkerbell Crane (8)
Westfields Junior School, Yateley

The Forbidden Castle

Four little children were desperate to discover the brilliant world of the castle. However, Uncle Alex said, 'No, beware, beware the castle of death. Many go in but none come out.' Once Uncle Alex had disappeared, the children and Rover ignored him and entered anyway. At first everything seemed normal but then two robbers appeared from the magical walls and chased them down the corridor. Rover could smell how to get away and guided the children out and to safety. The children were ashamed of themselves so went to find Uncle Alex to apologise. They now always listen to adults.

Ebony Grace Merritt (8)
Westfields Junior School, Yateley

Good Luck Jorja

Shh, Dad and Jorja are coming, hide... surprise! Today is Jorja's birthday and we want it to be perfect. My family don't have the best track record! One year Dad came home carrying my cake and tripped on a rubber duck and we ended up with cake everywhere, even on the ceiling. Another time, Mum had been so busy shopping for presents and getting food ready she had forgotten to invite anyone and nobody turned up! So for your first birthday Jorja I decided to take over and make it the best birthday ever. Happy birthday sis, I love you.

Jayden Ford (8)
Westfields Junior School, Yateley

Boldfang Meets An Alien

Boldfang was kicking his football around, bored, when he thought of something awesome! He dashed into his bedroom and, before you could say flapjack-jinks, he dived into his waste bin. 'Finally! It's made! Now for a test. Boosters? Check! Oxygen tank? Full! Food store? Loaded! I'm ready to launch my recycled rocket!' Blast-off! 'Wow, I'm here.'
As he got out, he heard strange chewing sounds. 'Munching aliens!' shrieked Boldfang. The aliens gave Boldfang a vegetable to eat, called heatroot. It was hotter than wasabi! Boldfang realised he could use it for fuel. So he did – and went home.

Elliot Casselton (8)
Westfields Junior School, Yateley

Guardians Of The Galaxy, Part 2

In a galaxy far, far away was a team who saved galaxies from the evil empire. In that team were the strongest, most intelligent characters in the universe called The Guardians of the Galaxy. One day on the planet Knowhere, the team were roaming around when they encountered evil villains, Thanos and Rohnin. Groot punched Rohnin into deep space, he never returned. Meanwhile the rest of the team were fighting Thanos. Groot lifted a rock and threw it making a deep hole to Knowhere's core. Thanos fell in and was blocked by the rock. Was that the end of him...?

Hudson Sherlock (8)
Westfields Junior School, Yateley

Lightning Strike

In an ordinary jungle there was an ordinary monkey. At lunchtime Coco and his friends had a race to see who could collect the most bananas. Coco was greedy and loved having the most bananas. At bedtime, Coco went out when everyone was asleep, to get some more bananas. On his way to the tree house it began to rain. Suddenly a lightning strike struck him. He lay on the floor, not knowing what was happening to him. He jumped up and found himself being able to fly and shoot bananas from his fingertips. He decided to be a superhero.

Reece Cole (8)
Westfields Junior School, Yateley

The Journey Of Ash

As Ash opened his eyes to be astonished, it was the day that he received his first Pokémon. Slipping his clothes on as fast as a cheetah, he ran, grabbed his bag of divine sweets. Luckily his mum was asleep in her cosy, soft bed. As he crept through the solid oak door he searched the area. He spotted Mindy. Mindy didn't recognise Ash for a moment but Ash shouted, 'Mindy!' They approached Professor Oak's lab. The two friends confidently chose a Pokémon. Mindy picked Bulhasaur but Ash selected Charmander. Now they are ready to start an adventure.

Harry Glossop (8)
Westfields Junior School, Yateley

The Dragon Who Liked Ice Cream Sundaes

There was a young dragon called Vector who lived in a forest with his parents. They had warned him not to leave the forest because he would scare people. One day he was curious about what was beyond the forest. While his parents were busy, Vector snuck to the edge of the forest. There he spotted a cottage with two children playing in the garden. They noticed Vector and said, 'Hello dragon we're Tilly and Alfie, would you like an ice cream sundae?' 'Yes please,' said Vector. So they all enjoyed some delicious ice cream and no one was scared.

Luke Fontaine (8)
Westfields Junior School, Yateley

The Video Game

'Yes... the highest score in the game,' yelled Bob, as he wearily rubbed his eyes. As he slowly opened his eyes again, he saw the World of Pixel and there in front of him stood a giant Cyclops. 'Let's do this!' yelled Bob, 'I've got all my weapons!' With a punch and a kick, the beast was gone. The sound of the game hitting the highest score for defeating the Cyclops rung in Bob's ears. He rubbed his eyes again, but this time when he opened them all he saw in front of him was his blank blue video game screen!

Rohan Wilson (8)
Westfields Junior School, Yateley

Adventure Of Jon Potter

I woke up in a mysterious basement. I didn't know where I was. The only thing I remember was going to potion class with Tyrone and Ronan. I rubbed my eyes to see my surroundings and saw a chained door with a sign saying: *Do Not Enter.* Carefully I stood up and crept silently to open the jet-black door... Behind the door I saw a metallic perilous dragon. All of a sudden it gobbled me up! Tyrone and Ronan immediately rushed to my aid and summoned an orbital strike that obliterated the dragon.

Jonathan Lai (8)
Westfields Junior School, Yateley

The Secret Library Adventure!

It was a normal school day, Jack and his friends were in the school library. Jack found an old book. When he touched it the bookcase moved and revealed an ancient door. The bell rang for break time. Outside Harry tripped over and found an old key. The friends went back in the library and touched the book. They turned the key in the lock and the door opened. Behind the door was an abandoned classroom full of old equipment, dust and cobwebs. They told their teacher and the school turned it into an awesome museum for everyone to enjoy.

Jack Watkin (8)
Westfields Junior School, Yateley

Mystery Pony

'Come on Ella,' said Jude.
'Wait Jude I hear something.' Ella ran towards the noise and there stood the most beautiful pony the girls had ever seen. 'Don't run, you will scare her,' said Jude.
'She is hurt, quick, we'd better get Mum.' The girls ran all the way through the paddock to the house. But when they returned to the pony she had gone. 'She must have got scared girls, don't worry we will keep a look out for her,' said Mum. As they walked home they heard her again. She was back. The girls didn't understand.

Grace Louise Hughes (8)
Westfields Junior School, Yateley

To The Rescue

A teenager named Emelia, was walking home from college. She looked over the hedge because she heard a distressed horse neighing. It seemed to her that it was Cloudier from her riding stable but who were the people and why were they so mean? Emelia had to think fast and went home and got her bike. When she got to the stable she said, 'Is Cloudier missing?'
They said, 'Yes.'
Emilia said, 'I know where she is.' She led the people from the stable to where Cloudier was but will they be in time? Yes they were, to save Cloudier.

Zoe Boorman (8)
Westfields Junior School, Yateley

Sophie's Adventure

Once upon a time Sophie did not know what she wanted to do when she grew up. 'I know, I would like to become a teacher.' Sophie went out to play and discovered a time travel machine in the park. Sophie decided to get in it and go forward twenty-two years in time, to her thirtieth birthday and discovered what her life was like. Thankfully when she got to the future she found she had a very happy life and her dream of becoming a teacher had come true. Sophie was so excited, she jumped about happily, smiling widely.

Cara James (8)
Westfields Junior School, Yateley

Lost On A Tropical Island

On a tropical island lived a fabulous, wonderful little girl called Micah. Micah, wore a long robe made of vines and grass. She also had azure eyes that glittered like gems!

One extremely horrid day Micah was taking a walk and spotted a thing hiding behind a rock. She looked behind it and found a guinea pig. 'Greetings,' said the guinea pig, 'I'm Pearl.'

Micah was astonished, 'You can talk. I'm a bit lost, can you help me find camp?'

'Sure.'

The two set off. Micah and Pearl had great adventures getting to know each other. They stayed together forever.

Micah Blignaut (7)
Westfields Junior School, Yateley

Blossom The Ocean Fairy

Once there was a fairy called Blossom the ocean fairy. She loved nothing more than spending her time by the water's edge. In the azure blue sky the sun was searing down. While Blossom was flying over the crystal-clear ocean, her wonderful wings got stuck in an old fishing net. Struggling to free herself, Sandy the starfish appeared. Sandy saw that Blossom was upset. She asked her what was the matter? Sandy hurried to get Melody the mermaid. Melody the musical mermaid hopped out of the ocean and untangled Blossom's wings. Blossom was free! Gracefully she rapidly glided home.

Mollie Marie Cole (8)
Westfields Junior School, Yateley

Discover An Animal

There's a boy called Alfie and a woman called Mandy. They went to a jungle exploring. Whilst exploring they came across a fierce huge animal. Interestingly the fierce animal has huge razor-sharp jaws. It wanted to be their friend. He didn't seem fierce to Alfie and to be his friend he gave him some food and the keeper of the jungle let Alfie go in with food. Amazingly Alfie and Mandy played with him and they were friends. Suddenly it was time to go home so they had to say goodbye. They're going to miss him.

Alfie David-Carter (8)
Westfields Junior School, Yateley

Layabout

We all love a happy ending to a story, but this one may surprise you!
There was once a young spindly boy who cared for the king's sheep. His Highness always warned, 'Don't fall asleep!'
Out in the field the boy strained, 'One, two, three.' And in the hope to become strong, he fell from the tree. Chin-ups were easy, or so he thought. 'I'll give up and go to sleep; surely I won't get caught.'
He was right, the king never found out. But what's the point, if all you become is a layabout?

Jacob Jay Matthews (7)
Westfields Junior School, Yateley

A Gorilla Stole My Mum!

Once upon a time there was a boy called Max who was exploring the Amazon rainforest with his mum. All of a sudden his mum was taken. He searched everywhere and found this gorilla. He asked Max would he like to learn the ways of a gorilla. Max said yes. So he told him everything he knew. His mum was revealed and they lived happily ever after.

James Wareham (8)
Westfields Junior School, Yateley

The Ruby Banana

Dave, the minion, said , 'Respect the banana!'
Spider-Man said, 'OK!' When they jumped into the machine and pushed the button, the next moment the door opened and they had landed in the Great Sphinx. They were in Ancient Egypt to find the ruby banana. They went a bit further and came up to a maze and Spider-Man went to the left and Dave went to the right and got lost. Spider-Man looked behind and shot a web. Dave turned back and went to the left and saw Spider-Man's web. They headed for the exit and saw the ruby banana...

Alfie Sydney Houlihan-Cook (7)
Westfields Junior School, Yateley

The Lost Ring

Rufus and three friends went on a diving trip in America. Rufus dived first into the turquoise water. They found a large cave filled with coral of all different colours. Rufus noticed something caught in the coral. It was a purse, and inside they found a signet ring engraved with a coat of arms. When they got back to the hotel they searched on the Internet and found the coat of arms belonged to a family called Clutterbuck. Only one member of the family was alive. They travelled to Washington to return the ring to grateful Mary Clutterbuck

Sophie Grace Greener (8)
Westfields Junior School, Yateley

Travelling To A Different Planet

Once there was a boy called Jamie. He lived in a mansion with a friend called Chris. Jamie liked exploring other worlds. The following night he dreamed about a world, it was hot and had different animals. He thought when he was older he wanted to explore the world .
Ten years later he got in a rocket and flew to space. On this world were lots of trees, bees, parrots and last of all monkeys swinging from tree to tree through the new world. Jamie and Chris were clueless for a name for this new world. Then they said, 'Rockwood!'

Lucas Santos (7)
Westfields Junior School, Yateley

Football Destruction

The second half is about to start but Bob wasn't on the pitch. Larry went to investigate. Bob was nowhere to be found but suddenly Larry heard a cry for help from the windmill. Larry went running to see but tripped on a rock and found a glowing stone. He picked it up and there was a flash in the sky and Larry turned into a superhero. He flew to the windmill to find Bob captured by two-faced Tony. Larry beat Tony in a fight and used his new super powers to rescue Bob so they could finish their match.

Matthew Plowman (8)
Westfields Junior School, Yateley

What A Great Day!

Benji was riding on his motorbike when he went to a motorcross track. When he arrived he saw his friends Joe and Ben who were also on their motorbikes. The three mates all lined up together ready to race each other when the gate goes down. Joe was the quickest off the mark followed by Ben then Benji. They all rode extremely well. By the end of the race, in first place was Joe, in second place was Ben and Benji came in third place. After the race they all went home and washed their motorbikes. What a great day!

Alfie Taplin (8)
Westfields Junior School, Yateley

The Big Matches

Once there was a boy named Henry and he played for Hawley FC. On the 21st June Hawley had a match against Camberly FC at 10. Hawley won that game 5-3. Then on the 28th June, Hawley had a match against, Cove. In the five minutes into the game Henry got fouled really badly in the box. The player got a red card and Henry won a penalty. Sadly Henry couldn't take the penalty because he was off the pitch but they won anyway.

Henry Neville (8)
Westfields Junior School, Yateley

The Map

In the deep, dark woods there was a little girl called Rapunzel and she was a princess. Then she found a map on the ground and a little note as well. She read the note and map and it said to Rapunzel, *There is a map to lead you to two places: the three little pigs or the lion king. But beware of the wolf in both. By your mother.* Then she said, 'Why would my mother write that?' She went to the little pigs and saw the wolf and defeated him with her long hair and he ran home terrified.

Jessica Hayden (8)
Westfields Junior School, Yateley

Untitled

Once upon a time there were three boys and the boys were football players. Their names were Dylan, Sanchez and Giroud. After that, some dinosaurs found a teleporter and one of them teleported to England and took Giroud. So Sanchez and Dylan had to save him from the dinosaurs. They found a teleporter and teleported to the dinosaur land. Once they got there they could see him but they couldn't get him. They had to climb a tree to get him. So they did it and got him and sprinted to the teleporter and went back home.

Dylan Clements (7)
Westfields Junior School, Yateley

What A Dream!

Silence was broken by a big bang coming from Mia's cupboard. She woke up and crept to her cupboard only to find a toy dinosaur. She curiously wondered how the toy could make such a loud bang, when suddenly she felt all dizzy. Then, found herself in a dry place apart from a few turquoise rivers and some puddles. *Thump! Thump! Thump!* She heard as she sensed that the ground was starting to shake madly. She ran to what looked like some little building which was a time machine. She jumped in. Then she found herself in bed fast asleep!

Beth Nwachukwu (8)
Westfields Junior School, Yateley

YOUNG WRITERS INFORMATION

We hope you have enjoyed reading this book – and that you will continue to in the coming years.

If you're a young writer who enjoys reading and creative writing, or the parent of an enthusiastic poet or story writer, do visit our website www.youngwriters.co.uk. Here you will find free competitions, workshops and games, as well as recommended reads, a poetry glossary and our blog.

If you would like to order further copies of this book, or any of our other titles, give us a call or visit **www.youngwriters.co.uk.**

Young Writers, Remus House
Coltsfoot Drive, Peterborough, PE2 9BF

(01733) 890066 / 898110
info@youngwriters.co.uk